"Raymond Chandler and Jim Thompson return from the dead, go on a month-long drinking binge, then hole up in a boardinghouse to write a book together. Six months later, they emerge, stinking of whiskey and tobacco, with a manuscript that would look a lot like *Dope*. Gran doesn't just copy this brawny style; she makes it her own. She's Chandler on steroids . . . the first great noir novel from a woman. The plot unfolds with more betrayals and twists than Thompson ever thought of stuffing into his warped masterpiece, *The Killer Inside Me*."                                —The Associated Press

A thrilling, heartbreaking journey through the heroin underbelly of 1950s New York. I was more than hooked. I was blown away."

—Richard Rayner,
author of *The Devil's Wind*

"Gran writes tight, with the muscular, vinegary style of a really good pulp novelist. [A] pitch-black mystery . . . a Weegee photograph in words . . . unsentimental to its clammy core."                —*The Washington Post*

"Dope just keeps on twisting." —*St. Louis Post-Dispatch*

"Dark and brooding in the best tradition of noir."
—*New York Daily News*

*continued . . .*

"Stark and utterly compelling. Entering the world of *Dope* . . . is like stepping into a favorite film noir, all black and white and ominous shades of gray . . . unraveling its way to a totally shocking—and perfect—conclusion. Readers will lift their eyes from these black-and-white pages, shocked to find so much color in the world, knowing that they should have seen that ending coming, but they never would have."           —*The Times-Picayune*

A heck of a book."                    —*Fort Worth Star-Telegram*

"Probably the year's scariest novel. *Come Closer* is the kind of novel that demands to be read on a wintry night in front of a log fire. It works insidiously, by undermining your sense of the world as something knowable and secure."                    —*Time Out*

"Amazingly scary . . . A story that will frighten the toughest cynics, make the hairs on the back of your neck stand on end and even keep you awake at night with fear."                    —*Coventry Evening Telegraph*

"An intelligent horror story, a literary creepshow. It worms its way under your skin and stays there."

—Darin Strauss,
author of *Chang and Eng*

*continued . . .*

*Titles by Sara Gran*

**DOPE**

**COME CLOSER**

**SATURN'S RETURN TO NEW YORK**

# DOPE

## Sara Gran

BERKLEY BOOKS, NEW YORK

**THE BERKLEY PUBLISHING GROUP**
Published by the Penguin Group
**Penguin Group (USA) Inc.**
**375 Hudson Street, New York, New York 10014, USA**
Penguin Group (Canada), 90 Eglinton Avenue East, Suite 700, Toronto, Ontario M4P 2Y3, Canada
(a division of Pearson Penguin Canada Inc.)
Penguin Books Ltd., 80 Strand, London WC2R 0RL, England
Penguin Group Ireland, 25 St. Stephen's Green, Dublin 2, Ireland (a division of Penguin Books Ltd.)
Penguin Group (Australia), 250 Camberwell Road, Camberwell, Victoria 3124, Australia
(a division of Pearson Australia Group Pty. Ltd.)
Penguin Books India Pvt. Ltd., 11 Community Centre, Panchsheel Park, New Delhi—110 017, India
Penguin Group (NZ), 67 Apollo Drive, Mairangi Bay, Auckland 1310, New Zealand
(a division of Pearson New Zealand Ltd.)
Penguin Books (South Africa) (Pty.) Ltd., 24 Sturdee Avenue, Rosebank, Johannesburg 2196,
South Africa

Penguin Books Ltd., Registered Offices: 80 Strand, London WC2R 0RL, England

This is a work of fiction. Names, characters, places, and incidents either are the product of the author's imagination or are used fictitiously, and any resemblance to actual persons, living or dead, business establishments, events, or locales is entirely coincidental. The publisher does not have any control over and does not assume any responsiblity for author or third-party websites or their content.

PRINTING HISTORY
G. P. Putnam's Sons hardcover edition / February 2006
Berkley trade paperback edition / February 2007

Berkley trade paperback ISBN: 978-0-425-21436-7

Library of Congress Cataloging-in-Publication Data

Gran, Sara.
Dope / Sara Gran.
p. cm.
ISBN 0-399-15345-4
1. Young women—Fiction.  2. Drug addicts—Fiction.  3. Missing persons—Fiction.  4. New York
(N.Y.)—Fiction.  5. College students—Fiction.  I. Title.
PS3607.R362D66      2006                2005053473
813'.6—dc22

PRINTED IN THE UNITED STATES OF AMERICA

10  9  8

# Chapter One

"Josephine."

Maude said my name flatly, like I was dead or she wanted me to be. I sat across from her at a booth in the back of the bar, where the daylight never reached and the smell of stale beer and cigarettes never cleared. Maude had been the mistress of a gangster back in the thirties and he'd bought her this bar to set her up with something after he was gone. It was on the corner of Broadway and West Fourth, and if you'd never been there before it would take a minute to notice that there wasn't a girl in the place, other than Maude. And now me. It was a queer joint. She let the boys hang out here because it was good business—it's not like they had too many other places to go—and of course there was an even better business in keeping their secrets.

"Hiya Maude." She looked at me as if I were speaking

another language. Pink lipstick was smeared on her lips, and she was squeezed into a gold strapless dress two sizes too small. Her hair was done up in a big blond pouf on top of her head.

I reached into my purse and pulled out a gold ring with a small diamond in a plain setting. An engagement ring. It was good. I'd boosted it from Tiffany's the day before.

I handed the ring to Maude. She grabbed it with her fat white hand, and then got out a magnifying glass from her pocketbook and looked the ring over, holding it up so it caught the yellow light coming from the bulb on the wall. She took her time. I didn't mind. Someone put a song on the jukebox. A few men started to dance with each other, but the bartender yelled at them to stop. They gave it up and went back to their seats. If the cops came in and saw dancing, everyone in the place would be locked up.

Maude looked the ring over a few more times and then looked up at me and said, "Fifty."

"I could do better in a pawnshop," I said. I couldn't hit Tiffany's every day and I wanted a good price. I wanted this ring to feed me for a month.

"Then do it," she said.

I held out my hand for the ring. She tapped it on the table, looking at me. We went through this every time.

"One hundred," she said.

I kept my hand where it was. She looked at the ring

and fondled it a little. Black makeup spread out around her eyes when she blinked.

"One fifty," she finally said.

I nodded. She reached into her little gold pocketbook and counted out seven twenties and a ten and rolled them up tight. She handed the money to me under the table. I counted it and then put the roll in my purse.

"Thanks, Maude," I said.

She didn't say anything. I stood up to go, and then she said, "Hey. If you see Shelley, you can tell her not to show her face around here no more."

I looked at her and sat back down. "What's the problem?"

"I ain't got a problem," Maude said. "Not with you. But Shelley, she brought me a bracelet, swore up and down it had a real emerald in it. Later I found out it was paste. She ain't welcome here no more."

"She must have thought—"

"I don't care what she thought," Maude said. "It was paste. I don't care if the King of Siam gave it to her. If you see her, tell her I don't want to see her again."

I sighed. "All right," I said. "If I pay it off, you'll help her out the next time she's in a jam?"

Maude nodded. "I don't hold grudges, Josephine. You know that."

"Okay," I said, feeling heavy. "What'd she burn you for?"

"Two hundred," Maude said.

"You never gave anyone two hundred dollars in your life," I said. "Not even if it *was* the King of Siam." We haggled all over again for a while. Finally we agreed that one twenty-five would cover it, and I handed back over most of the money she'd just given me. I stood up and left. Ordinarily I would have stayed and played a bit of pool—some of the queers were good, and I liked to stay in practice—but I had an appointment downtown.

# Chapter Two

The bright sun outside was a shock after Maude's. It was one o'clock in the afternoon on May 14, 1950, in New York City. On Broadway I hailed a taxi to take me down to Fulton Street, and then I walked a few blocks until I found number 28. It was quite a place, a tall narrow building that looked like someone had poured it in between the two buildings on either side. The whole front of it was white stone carved up with clouds and faces and stars, and it came to a point at the top like a church. A doorman in a sharp blue uniform with gold braid opened the door for me with a big smile. Inside there were marble floors with clean red rugs and streams of people coming in and out, busy people in suits with briefcases and very important places to go. In the middle of the lobby was a big marble counter where a good-looking fellow in the same uniform sat guiding everyone on their busy way. But I already knew where I was going.

An elevator man in another blue suit and another big smile brought me up to five. On the fifth floor there were four mahogany doors set into mahogany paneling, each with a shiny brass doorknob and a frosted window with the name of the company painted in gold and outlined in black. Painted on the first door was *Jackson, Smith and Alexander, Attorneys-at-Law*. The next was *Beauclair, Johnson, White and Collins, Attorneys*. The third was *Piedmont, Taskman, Thompson, Burroughs, Black and Jackson, Law Office*.

The last door had nothing on it. That was the one I was looking for.

It was open. Inside was a waiting room with a pretty brunette girl in a white suit and black-rimmed eyeglasses sitting behind a desk. There was a beautiful red Persian rug on the floor and two ugly oil paintings of landscapes on the walls. Three oversized leather armchairs were set around a low wood table that had copies of *Forbes* magazine fanned out on it.

The girl smiled at me. I didn't smile back. I was tired of smiling.

"I'm here to see Mr. Nathaniel Nelson," I said. "We have an appointment. Josephine Flannigan."

"Certainly, Miss Flannigan."

She hopped up out of her chair and led me through a door behind her. On the other side was a corner office room about five times the size of the room I lived in. Here was an even bigger desk and a lot more leather furniture and a man and a woman. The man sat behind the desk. He was about forty-five, with silver hair and big brown eyes, and wore a dark gray suit that looked like it had been custom made for him. He looked tired, but had a strong jaw and a square face that looked like it wouldn't take no for an answer, like he had been the boss for so long he forgot he wasn't really the boss of anything at all.

I took a deep breath, and inhaled the smell of money.

The woman sat to the left of the desk. She was about forty and didn't look like much at all. She was pretty enough, if you didn't like personality in your women. She had blond hair pulled back from her face in a plain, perfect chignon. She wore a black suit that showed nothing and didn't seem to be hiding much of anything at all, and too much makeup over a face that looked just this side of being alive.

"Mr. Nelson," I said. "How do you do. I'm Josephine Flannigan."

He stood up, leaned across the table, and shook my hand. He was taller than I thought he'd be, taller and wider. "How do you do, Miss Flannigan. This is my wife, Maybelline Nelson."

She stood up and I took her hand. It was limp.

The girl left and closed the door behind her and we all sat down. I took off my gloves and put them across my lap. Mrs. Nelson rested her eyes on something ten feet past me and over my left shoulder. Mr. Nelson looked at me and opened his mouth but I spoke first. I knew his type. If I let him take hold of the conversation, I'd never get it back.

"So, Mr. Nelson, who was it that gave you my phone number?"

"Nick Paganas," he said. I looked blank so he added: "I think you know him as Nick the Greek."

I smiled. I knew at least a dozen guys who went by Nick the Greek, but it wouldn't do any good to let him know that. "Sure, Nick," I said. "How do you know him?"

He looked down at the table and frowned. Then I knew how he knew Nick the Greek. But he told me anyway: "Mr. Paganas—he took me for quite a bit of money, Miss Flannigan."

"Stocks?" I guessed.

Mr. Nelson shook his head. "Real estate. He sold me fifty acres of land in Florida. Eventually I realized I had bought a nice chunk of the Atlantic Ocean."

"Sure," I said. I tried not to smile. "He's a professional, Mr. Nelson. He's fooled a lot of men of very high stature—you'd be surprised if I told you who." I didn't know who, exactly, we were talking about, but it was probably true. "What I mean is, you're in very good company."

Mrs. Nelson kept her eyes straight ahead, on whatever ghost she was staring at.

"Thank you, Miss Flannigan. That's a kind thing to say. Anyway, fortunately I realized this before Mr. Paganas left town, so I was able to recoup my losses. And something else. I told Mr. Paganas that I wouldn't report him to the police on one condition. If he would help me find my daughter."

"And he recommended me?"

"Yes. He recommended you," Mr. Nelson answered. "He said you no longer used drugs, that you were honest, that we could trust you. He said you knew—well, you knew the type of places where she might be. You see . . ." He paused and looked at his wife. She pulled her eyes out of the void and looked back at him. He turned to me again. "My daughter is on drugs, Miss Flannigan. My daughter is a . . . *a dope fiend.*"

I held back a laugh. I read the papers: every square in America these days thought their kid was a dope fiend. Mostly from what I gathered their kids smoked a little tea and cut school once in a while. And the paperback novels were full of them—kids who started off popping a benny and ended up on heroin, murdering a dozen of their neighbors with their bare hands. Kids from nice families who got lured in by evil pushers. On the book covers, the pushers always had mustaches.

I had never met an addict who came from a nice home. I'd met addicts who came from families that had money and nice houses. But never from a nice home. And I'd never met a dealer who had a mustache.

"Tell me about your daughter," I said.

He sighed. "Nadine. About a year ago—"

"How old is she now?" I asked.

"Eighteen."

"Nineteen," the mother cut in. She said it slowly, like it had only just occurred to her what was going on here.

"Yes, nineteen," Mr. Nelson continued. "About a year ago—"

"It started before that," Mrs. Nelson interrupted. She looked directly at me for the first time. "She started going into the city on the weekends with her friends."

"Where do you live?" I asked.

"Westchester."

"Ah."

She continued: "She started going into the city with her girlfriends every weekend. Didn't want to go to the club, didn't want to see her old friends anymore. Nothing so wrong with that. She was in her last year of high school."

Mr. Nelson picked up the story. "Except she started coming home—well, we thought she was drunk."

"Now, of course," Mrs. Nelson said, "we're not so sure."

"She started coming home later and later. Drunk or whatever she was."

"It seemed normal," Mrs. Nelson pointed out. "She was a young girl and she wanted to have fun. She wanted to spend some time in the city."

"She wanted to go to Barnard," Mr. Nelson said. "So she went to Barnard. We thought . . . You can imagine. We thought she'd get it out of her system after a few years of living in the city. Sow her wild oats and then get married or even start a career, whatever would make her happy."

"She always loved to draw," Mrs. Nelson said. "I thought she might like to work in fashion or advertising or something like that. It might be fun for her."

"But that didn't happen?" I asked.

"No," Mr. Nelson answered. "No. Instead we got complaints from the dorm mother, then from the dean. Nadine was coming home late, staying out, failing her classes."

"Even art," Mrs. Nelson pointed out.

"Even art," Mr. Nelson agreed. "And she was avoiding us. We hardly ever saw her anymore. Finally one night it all exploded. The dorm mother found something in her room—a kit for injecting drugs."

"*Shooting up,*" Mrs. Nelson clarified. I nodded solemnly.

"We wanted to take her to the doctor," Mr. Nelson continued. "But she refused. It turns out there wasn't anything the doctor could do for her anyway. . . . Well, I'm sure you know about that."

I nodded again.

"She promised to stop on her own," Mr. Nelson said. "But she didn't. She couldn't. This went on for months. Finally, they had to expel her from school."

"That was when she left," Mrs. Nelson cut in. "The day she had to leave the dorm. We went to go pick her up—"

"She was going to come home with us."

"But she wasn't there. She had left the night before. Just left, in the middle of the night."

"We haven't heard from her since."

"How long ago was that?" I asked.

"Three months ago," Mrs. Nelson answered.

"And you're just starting to look now?"

They looked at each other, annoyed. "We've *been* looking," Mrs. Nelson said. "First we called the police—"

"They didn't care. They said they would look into it."

"We never heard from them again," Mrs. Nelson continued. "That was the New York City police. Of course everyone in Westchester was very concerned, but there was nothing they could do. We tried looking around on our own, talking to her friends at school, trying to find out where—where people like that would be. But we got nowhere.

"So we hired a private investigator." Mrs. Nelson reached into her purse and pulled out a photograph. "He found out she was living with this man, Jerry McFall, in some little dump down on Eleventh Street. But by the time he told us about it, they were gone. He couldn't find them again."

She handed me the photo. A man and a girl were standing on Eleventh Street, near First Avenue. It was a sunny day. The girl was looking down at the ground. She had light hair and light eyes and small symmetrical features that didn't draw any attention. She was pretty, but only if you took the time to look. And there was nothing there to grab you and make you do that. Her hair was pulled back in a ponytail and she wore a tight black sweater with a black skirt and white high-heeled shoes. She looked like a cross between a college girl and a whore. And she didn't look happy.

The man didn't look happy, either. He wore a wide-brimmed hat and a fancy tweed suit. He looked like a pimp. He was thin and his face was long and narrow. I guessed he was a little younger than me, maybe thirty, give or take a few years. His eyes were dark and his hair was probably light brown. Not good-looking. Not ugly, either.

"What color are her eyes?" I asked.

"Blue," her mother answered. "Her hair is blond, like mine."

"How tall is she?"

"Five feet three," Mrs. Nelson said.

That would put the man at a little under six feet. He looked like he wanted to smack the girl.

"The investigator took that," she said.

"We fired him," Mr. Nelson added. "That was all he came up with. I don't think he had the connections."

"*Underworld* connections," Mrs. Nelson explained.

"What we mean is, we need someone who knows about drug addicts, and girl drug addicts in particular. What concerns us the most is that Nadine doesn't have any money."

"This man, Nick the Greek, he said that you would know where people like that go, how they make money and where they buy drugs and that sort of thing. You see, Nadine doesn't have any money—"

"We'd rather have her home, even as a drug addict, where we can keep our eyes on her and know that she's safe."

14

"We think you can find her," Mrs. Nelson said, looking at me. "We'd like to have her at home."

"We think you can find her, Miss Flannigan," Mr. Nelson repeated. "If you start looking today I'll give you a thousand dollars, cash, right now. And a thousand more if you find her. But that's to include all of your expenses, gasoline and meals and anything else you might incur—even travel."

A thousand dollars. Cash.

I looked from one to the other. They looked anxious and eager and hopeful. I knew they weren't telling me everything. Like I said, I'd never met a dope addict from a nice home. Maybe Mrs. Nelson hit the bottle, or maybe Mr. Nelson had a girl on the side, or five or ten girls. Maybe they spanked Nadine too much when she was a kid, or still did it, or gave her hell over her grades or were trying to get her to marry the guy from next door. Maybe the girl wasn't on drugs at all and just thought Westchester was a boring place to be and didn't want to go back there.

It didn't matter. With a thousand dollars up front, it didn't matter if I found her at all. If and when I found her I would worry about what to do with her.

I was walking out with a thousand dollars. That was what mattered.

"I have to be honest with you," I said. They already seemed ready to hand over the money but I figured it couldn't hurt to tighten the screws. "I've never done anything like this before. I'm not sure if I'm the right person for the job."

"I'm not sure, either," Mr. Nelson said. "Frankly, Miss Flannigan, all I know about you is that you live in New York City, you're . . . that you're in the same line of work as Mr. Paganas, and that you used to be a drug addict. But for now, you're our only hope."

I wasn't in the same line of work as Mr. Paganas, whoever he was, if he was selling real estate to Mr. Nelson. Not really. We'd probably started off in the same line of work, years ago, and while he moved up to selling real estate to people like Mr. Nelson, I'd moved down to boosting jewelry and pickpocketing. I figured he had recommended me because he didn't know any other dope addicts, and the whole business was probably not enough dough for anyone else he knew. I took in a deep breath and let it out slowly, looking from one to the other, like I was thinking.

"Okay," I said. "I'll do it."

They both looked like a weight had fallen off their shoulders. I told them the thousand would buy them a month. After that, if they wanted me to keep looking, they'd need to cough up more. I'd call them right away if I found anything, and if I didn't find anything I'd call them at the end of the week to check in. They agreed.

Mr. Nelson handed me an envelope with ten hundred-dollar bills inside.

"So you'll call," Mrs. Nelson said again before I left, her eyes begging me. "You'll call right away if you find out anything at all."

"Of course," I told her. "You can trust me."

# Chapter Three

'd never been to the campus of Barnard before, and after spending the morning there I didn't plan on ever going again. The buildings looked like courthouses, and the place was so far uptown I thought I was in Boston. The closest I'd been to it before was up to 103rd Street, where a fellow I knew sold junk in a cafeteria. When the subway had stopped there I'd almost gotten off the train out of habit.

It'd taken me most of the afternoon the day before to get an appointment with the dean of students. Now we were in his office, in one of the buildings that looked like a courthouse, a messy room with books everywhere and no fresh air. The dean was a skinny man in a cheap suit past middle age, with small narrow eyes and limp hands. It was hard to imagine anyone taking a look at this fellow and thinking, *Now* here's *a man I trust around a bunch of college coeds*. He remembered Nadine all right.

"A lovely girl," he said, more than once. "Really lovely."

"Right. I know. I've seen her picture. So you knew her well?"

"Not well," he said. "I don't get a chance to know any of the individual girls that well, unfortunately. But of course when she began having her problems, that was brought to my attention, and I spoke with her a few times."

"Oh yeah? What'd you talk about?" I wanted to get out of that stuffy room. Through the window I could see the sun shining outside. Green things were starting to grow all over the place and flowers were popping out every way you looked. The kids walking across campus were all smiling. It was hard to imagine the girl I'd seen in the photo here. She looked like another breed.

He took a long breath and let it out slowly. "Well, the nature of her problems, naturally. I mean, she was using drugs, and I advised her against it. I let her know the school's policy on that kind of thing."

"I'm sure that was very helpful to her," I said. "But did you try to get her into any kind of therapy? Get her into a hospital or anything like that?" None of those cures did a whole lot, but they were a little bit better then nothing. Especially for a young girl, not too far gone, like Nadine.

The dean of students looked at me with his small eyes. "Miss Flannigan, we have some problems we are ready to help our girls with. Homesickness, a little rebellion, trouble adjusting to the schoolwork—we even have a girl, occasionally, who drinks a little too much. But frankly, Nadine is the first drug addict I have ever met. It's not that I didn't want to help her. Of course I did. But that is simply beyond the scope of what we can deal with here. *That,*" he added firmly, as if he were convincing himself, "falls under the realm of what we would consider a family problem, not a problem for the school. I mean, *drugs.* On a college campus . . ." He lifted his hands up in the air and tried to look sympathetic.

"How about the one who actually found the drugs in her room, the dorm mother?" I asked. "Could I speak with her?"

Miss Duncan, the dorm mother, weighed about four hundred pounds, and she hated the girls she was supposed to be watching. She lived in a room in the dormitory a little bigger than the rest, but not quite big enough for all that weight. We sat on her sofa together while Miss Duncan told me all about Nadine.

"Well, I had never had any experience with that kind of thing," she assured me. She wore a black dress that was very large, but still tight, and her eyebrows were drawn on in a high round arch, making her look surprised. "Not before I came here. But these girls . . ."

She let her voice trail off. I smiled. "College girls. I was certainly never one myself."

"Me either," Miss Duncan confided, in case I had any doubts. "I mean, what's the point? I mean, if you're going to *do something* with your education, sure. If you're going to do something. I mean, for someone like me, it would have been nice. I could have done something. But these girls—well, you know. They're all here getting their M-R-S degree. That's as far as it goes with them."

"Oh I know," I said. I had no idea what she was talking about. "Nadine's parents tell me she was interested in art. Did she spend a lot of time on that?"

Miss Duncan rolled her eyes. "Nadine was like the rest of them. Boys, parties, clothes—that was all she cared about."

"Did you know anything about her condition before you found works in her room?"

She looked at me for a minute. "Oh," she finally said. "You mean the syringe and all that. *Works.* No, I had no idea. Like I said, I didn't know anything about that kind of thing until I came here. These girls, they've given me quite an education, I can tell you that."

"I can imagine. Did you know her parents?"

Miss Duncan nodded. "They came by once a month or so. They're in Westchester, it's not far. They're one of those . . . you know. Very *prominent* families. The father is a very *prominent* lawyer in Manhattan. Of course all the girls here are from that type of a family. You know, ship the girl off to Barnard, have her meet the right people, that whole nine yards."

I asked her if I could speak to Nadine's roommate. It took some work, but she stood up and led me to a room on the second floor of the dorm, where the girl still lived by herself. Miss Duncan knocked once and then opened the door. It was a small, plain room with two single beds, two desks, and two dressers. One half of the room was obviously empty: no sheets on the bed, nothing on the desk, no knickknacks on top of the dresser. A young girl with red hair was sitting at the other desk writing in a notebook. She wore a plaid skirt with a white blouse and saddle shoes, and her skin was so white it almost blended in with the blouse.

Miss Duncan introduced us and explained that I was trying to find Nadine. The girl's name was Claudia. She smiled.

"Sure, anything I can do to help," she said. She sounded like she came from a farm. I sat down on the empty twin bed and stared at Miss Duncan until she left.

"So," I said to Claudia, once the dorm mother was gone. "You must have known Nadine pretty well. This is an awfully small room."

Claudia shrugged. "We weren't that close. I mean, we lived together and all, but mostly Nadine kept to herself."

"What was she like?"

Claudia wrinkled up her brow. "She was kind of moody. Kept to herself, like I said."

"She didn't go out a lot? Have boyfriends, go dancing?"

The girl shook her head. "No, she really wasn't like that at all. She liked to stay in the room a lot when she wasn't out with her friends. She didn't join any clubs or go to football games or anything like that."

"Who were her friends?" I asked.

"I don't know," Claudia said. "I know she had some friends down in the Village who she saw, but I don't know who they were. I guess she'd spent some time there before she started school. And then she had a regular fellow. Jerry something-or-other. I think by the time all that stuff happened, she was pretty much only spending time with him, and not seeing any of her other friends anymore. When she wasn't out with him, she sat around the room, mostly. Drawing. Oh, look—" She pointed at a sketch above her desk. It was a sketch of Claudia. I didn't know anything about art, but it looked an awful lot like Claudia. More than a photograph would have. "Nadine did that. She gave it to me. To be honest, she kind of got on my nerves. I mean, she wasn't very friendly, seeing as we were roommates and all. She never invited me to go out with her, never introduced me to her boyfriend. And when she was here, she just sat in bed and drew pictures. We never talked much. Of course now, well, I just feel so bad. . . ."

I looked at her. She felt pretty bad. "Did you know about the drugs?"

"Oh, no," she said, raising her eyebrows. "Before I came here, I had never even had a drink! Honestly, I never thought . . . I mean, I didn't even know that kind of stuff existed. What happened was, one night she didn't come home. I got worried, so I talked to Miss Duncan. Well, she comes in and starts poking around, and right in the top drawer of Nadine's desk there was all this stuff. A needle and drugs and all that. I didn't even know what it was until Miss Duncan explained it to me. I thought Nadine was sick or something, that it was some kind of medicine. So of course they had a big talk with her and called her parents and everything like that. But it didn't seem to help. It just got worse until she was hardly ever here at all and when she was, well, she wasn't much fun to be around. Then they expelled her, and after that I never saw her again. She left the night before her parents were supposed to come get her."

"You didn't see her leave?" I asked.

She shook her head. "I didn't even wake up."

Neither of us said anything for a minute. I hadn't learned much.

"I guess how she was so moody and all," Claudia

said. "I guess that was the drugs, huh?" She looked at me. I nodded.

"I guess once you start," she said slowly, as if she was just figuring everything out, "it's pretty hard to quit, isn't it?"

"Yes," I told her. "I've heard that it is."

# Chapter Four

That evening I met Jim Cohen for dinner at Lenny's, a seafood house in Little Italy. It was Jim's favorite restaurant and we ate there three or four times a month. I liked Lenny's, but my favorite was Lorenzo's. Jim wouldn't step foot in the place—he said the waiters were too slow and the hard rolls were too hard.

Jim was particular like that about everything. His suits were made by a Jewish guy on Orchard Street and he wouldn't get a suit anywhere else, and his hats could only come from Belton's on Delancey Street. His whiskey had to be Bushmills, his handkerchiefs had to be ironed so that they'd fold perfectly into his pocket, his shoes had to be new, from Florsheim's, and polished at least once a day. But Jim could afford to be particular. Before the war he used to sell dope by the pound, but when he came back there was no dope to sell. He did a little of this and a little of that for a while and then he got a regular thing going working with Chicago Gary. Gary sold stock tips and racetrack tips and land in Florida and shares in oil wells, a con man of the old school. He lived in Chicago, so he did a lot of work in New York—the con men had an arrangement with the police not to work where they lived. If he was in town and he needed a shill or a banker or an extra inside man, he called Jim. It was good work but it wasn't steady. Jim always made enough when he worked with Gary to last him until the next time, if he was smart, but he wasn't, not with money, so in between Gary's trips to New York he'd do a little of this and a little of that again.

Lenny was at the door when I came in. He was a nice enough guy but he always had his knickers in a knot about something. Worked too hard. He had six kids and he wanted them all to go to college. So far they'd all dropped out of high school. He had three left to try his luck on.

"Jim here yet?" I asked him.

"In the kitchen," he said, pointing at a door in the back with a sour face. "Please, get him out of there before the guys kill him."

I said I would give it a try. Sure enough, there was Jim, arguing with the cook over a big pot on the stove.

The guys who worked in the kitchen stood around and watched silently.

"Oregano!" Jim shouted. "There ain't any oregano in here!" Everyone watched as he tasted whatever was in the pot. Then he scowled like he might spit it out. "How come a goddamned Jew," he said, "a damn Jew from the Lower East Side has gotta come in here and tell you guys from Italy how to cook?"

First Vincent, the head cook, started to lose it. Next the other boys cracked up and soon they were all in hysterics.

"I mean where the hell are you guys really from, eh?" Jim yelled. "Vincent, how about you—you're a Polack, you gotta be, making crap like this in the kitchen." Vincent doubled over with laughter. "And you," he said to one of the line cooks, "you've gotta be Irish, you—"

He would have gone on all night but he saw me standing by the door. "Hey," he said, putting down his spoon. "Gentlemen, watch your language already. There's a lady in the room."

Of course that got another round of laughs because no one except Jim had said a word. Jim shook hands with the men and then followed me out of the kitchen and over to a table by the window in the dining room, where a platter of food was already laid out for us. Everyone at Lenny's loved Jim. He was their favorite customer.

Jim served us each baked clams and eggplant from the platter and then asked how my meeting with the Nelsons went. I told him all about it.

"Sounds good," he said, nodding his head. "How'd they find you?"

"They said Nick the Greek set it up."

He asked which Nick. I told him I didn't know, and we went over the possibilities of all the different Nicks for a while.

"Anyway," I said, "you know either of them?" I showed him the photo of McFall and Nadine.

Jim looked at the photo for a minute and then made a face. "Not the girl. But the man, yeah, I know him. Jerry Mc-Something, right?"

I nodded.

"I haven't seen him in five years, maybe," Jim said. Since Jim had left the business he hadn't had anything to do with junk or the people who sold it. Most of the fellows who used to know him thought Jim had gotten too big for his britches. He didn't care. Even though he'd never sold on the street, only by the pound, it still turned his stomach a little. He'd always hated the junkies and their dealers and had been happy to wash his hands of the whole business. "Sold some dope to him once, tried to rip me off for the payment. Never had anything to do with him again. How about you, you know him?"

"Yeah," I said. "I bought from him once. Real lowlife. He didn't just want money, if you know what I mean." Jim nodded. "Just once. I don't know why I even remember it." But I did know. Because he did what he wanted and afterward I felt kind of sick and I told myself, *This is the last time*. It wasn't, of course. But it was the beginning. Out of all the things I did for dope, that was the one I remembered the most, even though it only took a few minutes. Maybe it was the one that kept me from going back. "Anyway," I said, "I'm sure he doesn't remember me. And I don't know where he is now."

"So are you gonna find the girl," Jim asked, "or just take the thousand and forget about it?"

I thought about the one time I had met Jerry McFall. The girl was with him now. "Another thousand if I do. I might as well try."

Jim nodded. "Where are you gonna start?"

I told him what I had done so far, which was waste my time up at Barnard.

"You know who you ought to talk to," Jim said after a minute. "Old Paul. The guy who lives on the Bowery. If the girl's been using dope for a while, she'd be likely to meet him at some point, right?"

I nodded. It wasn't a bad idea.

"Oh, hey," Jim said. "Before I forget. There was a nice picture of Shelley in the *Daily News* today. An ad for a jewelry store on Fifth Avenue."

"Thanks," I said. "Was the ad for a bracelet, by the way?"

Jim nodded. "Yeah, you saw it?"

The waiter brought over plates of linguine with calamari and hard rolls.

"Hey, that reminds me," I said, changing the topic. "You seen Mick lately? Mick from the Bronx? I heard he got outta Rikers."

"Oh, yeah," Jim said. "He's been out for months now." He smiled. "In fact, I wasn't going to tell you this, but I bought a dress for you off him just yesterday. Straight from Bergdorf's. It's a real knockout. You're gonna love it."

We talked some more and finished dinner and then had glasses of sweet wine before we left. After dinner I usually went back to Jim's place with him, but I was tired that evening and wanted to go home. We said goodnight outside the restaurant and I walked through Little Italy for a while before I got a taxi. There were a few tourists walking around, leaving restaurants or looking for one. Groups of teenagers went from block to block, seeing what the news was on the various street corners. Kids were playing stickball in the street. A woman yelled from a tenement window: "Ant'ny! Ant'ny, you come home RIGHT NOW!"

At Houston Street I stopped at a newsstand and bought the *Daily News*. Then I got a taxi to take me the rest of the way home. I lived in the Sweedmore, a hotel for women on Twenty-second and Second. My room was around the size of a shoebox, but it was safe and clean. Lavinia, the old lady who ran the place, spent most of her life at the front desk scowling at the girls who lived there and finding reasons to throw us out. She was okay. That was her job. She scowled at me when I came in. I scowled back and went up to my room and took off the god-awful suit I had put on for the dean of students and put on a pair of men's pajamas.

I sat down in an old armchair, one of two I had got secondhand to furnish the place. The bed and the dresser had come with the room. I had bought the armchairs and a little table in the corner for a hot plate and a per-colator, and there was a coffee table that a girl down the hall gave me when she moved out. On the floor was an old phonograph and some 78 records. The bathroom was down the hall, shared with three other girls.

When I got my room at the Sweedmore I'd just stopped using dope and just got out of jail, and I didn't have a penny. Early in the evening, after the banks closed, I gave Lavinia a check to hold the place. The check came from a checkbook that I'd lifted from a lady's handbag on the subway, and I knew she'd cancel it as soon as she noticed it was gone. So I spent the rest of the night back on the subway, relieving the riders of their wallets, until I had enough for the rent and some extra to eat and buy clothes besides. It got easier as the night went on and people started to come home from clubs drunk and come home from working the night shift exhausted. I worked until eight the next morning and then I met Lavinia in the lobby before she went to the bank. She didn't mind ripping up the check and taking cash instead.

I sat in the armchair and thought about pouring myself a bourbon, but I didn't. A lot of people got off dope just to get hooked on booze or coke or pills, and I was trying not to let that happen. Instead I went to the closet and took down a wooden cigar box from the top shelf. Inside was a little bit of weed and a packet of cigarette papers. I rolled a stick for myself and lit it up. I didn't worry about weed. You never got hooked. It just helped you sleep.

I looked through the paper. There on page five was Shelley, a close-up of her head and shoulders, with her hands crossed right under her neck. She was wearing a pair of big earrings and a necklace and bracelet to match, all dripping with jewels. Paste, apparently, but it did look good. No wonder they'd let her take off with the bracelet.

From the top drawer of the dresser I got a big black scrapbook and a pair of scissors and some glue and took it all back to the armchair. I looked through the scrapbook. On the first page was a photo of Shelley in satin shorts and a little checked top tied at the waist. It was from a crime magazine, her first modeling job. She was supposed to be the victim of the Pillowcase Strangler. Her hair was darker then and she was still skinny then, like a kid. That was over ten years ago. I'd been so proud of her when it came out that I'd nicked a solid silver key chain from Alexander's for her.

Next was a picture from *Real Confessions*. She was wearing a cotton dress and her mouth was open in a big scream. I didn't read the story that went along with that one—raped by her neighbor, I think. After that were more pictures from magazines, her first few advertisements, and then some playbills from shows she'd been in. They hadn't been big parts, just the chorus line or small roles without lines, like The Maid or Girl Number Two. Still, they were Broadway shows.

Toward the end was an ad for a show at a supper club on the East Side. Don Holiday and his Christmas Magic. Shelley was a dancing elf. I'd seen the show and afterward I'd gone backstage. Shelley could only talk for a minute, though, because Don Holiday was waiting to take her out to dinner. That was the last time I'd seen her.

I cut out the new photo and pasted it into the last blank page. Then I smoked a little more weed and went to bed. Tea might not hook you, but sometimes it gave you crazy dreams. That night I dreamed of Mr. and Mrs. Nelson chasing Jerry McFall around and around the big expensive rug in Nelson's office. I stood off to the side, wondering when I could step in and tag him and claim my thousand bucks.

# Chapter Five

Paul had a big place on the Bowery that he'd had ever since the war ended and dope had become easy to get again. While the war was on and for a few years afterward the only way to get it was scripts; find yourself a croaker who'd write you a prescription for morphine or some other junk and then find a druggist stupid enough or poor enough to fill the script. But since then dope had flooded the streets again and the going was good, and getting better every day. I sure had picked a dumb time to give it up. A dumb time to get arrested and serve thirty days in the Women's House of Detention doing cold turkey, two years ago now. I spent all of the war and the hard times afterward running around from doctor to drugstore and back again, and now you could buy the stuff on practically any street corner in Harlem and through plenty of easy connections downtown.

It wasn't the first time I'd quit. I'd gotten off dope plenty of times before, sometimes for weeks or months, once for almost a year. Bur this time, I was doing things differently. Like not using drugs, for example. That seemed to help with the quitting. And not being around dope and people who used it so much. That helped, too. Which was why I hadn't seen Paul in two years.

The Bowery was empty except for a handful of drunks scattered around, arguing about where their next drink was coming from. A man and a woman huddled in the doorway of Paul's building, counting out change for a bottle of wine. They looked at me hopefully. I shook my head before they had a chance to ask. Across the street was a man in a neat pin-striped suit and a gray fedora, watching Paul's building. Probably a husband or a boyfriend looking for his girl, waiting for her to come out so he could take her home. He wouldn't go inside, if he was smart. Paul had a good friend in the DA's office from their old college days and they had a deal: anything that went on in the place on the Bowery was home free. Once Paul was outside, though, he was fair game. So he didn't go out much.

The couple slowly moved out of the doorway, shaking and muttering, and I went in. The hallway was wide and dark and smelled like piss. I walked up to the third floor. Paul's door was open so I let myself in. It was a big railroad apartment with no doors between the rooms.

The place was quiet and smelled stale. You entered into the kitchen, which was empty except for the built-in fixtures. If someone had figured out how to take out the sink and sell it for dope, it wouldn't be there, either. As it was, the Frigidaire, the table, the chairs, the china, and everything else were gone.

I'd spent a few days at Paul's myself, or maybe it was weeks. Or months. After I'd split from my husband I'd planned to clean up but it didn't work out that way, not at first. Paul didn't ask for much, just that you kept yourself looking decent and made yourself available and didn't complain. Any girlfriends you had were always welcome, although I didn't have any left by then. Paul got on my nerves after a while and so I left with a fellow I met there, a friend of his named Steve. I should have stuck with Paul.

I went through to the next room. Two girls sat on the floor in the corner, nodding out. Their eyes were closed and they were slouched over, leaning against each other like rag dolls. Otherwise the room was empty. I went over to the girls and crouched down. One of them, a blonde, heard me come over and used all her strength to pull her eyes open and bring her head upright. She was pretty and young and thin, wearing a nice brown dress and brown alligator shoes. When she saw me she nudged her friend, trying to get her up. Her friend was a little trashier looking, and not as pretty. She wore a tight black skirt, pulled up over her knees, and a tight pink sweater, with black hair done up high on her head.

"Where's Paul?" I said to the blonde. She tried to smile, but it came out crooked. "Paul," I said. "Where's Paul?" She made a move that was kind of like a shrug, with the broken crooked smile still on her face.

I stood up and walked into the next room. This room was smaller than the one before and it was also empty. The door to the bathroom was here. It was open, and through the doorway I saw a man around my age, in a tattered brown suit, cleaning out a set of works at the sink. When he saw me looking he got angry and slammed the door.

I went through to the last room. Paul was sitting on the floor with another young girl, another blonde. He was just pulling a needle out of her arm when he heard me come in, and he finished what he was doing before he turned around to face me. The girl looked around for a minute, not saying anything, and then she turned away from me, toward the window. Maybe she thought that if she couldn't see me, I couldn't see her.

Paul smiled at me. "Joey. Welcome back." His voice was hoarse like an old man's.

"Thanks," I said. "How you doing, Paul?"

"Can't complain."

He stood up, a tall thin skeleton in a Brooks Brothers shirt and custom-made slacks. Paul had money from a family in Kansas or Missouri or someplace like that, which paid for this apartment and his fancy clothes and dope for him and an endless stream of girls.

"Sit down, Joey, let me set you up." I looked down at the floor. Next to the girl was a pile of brown powder on a piece of paper. The pile was about as big as a half dollar and almost as high.

They say once you've been an addict your biology is never the same. All your cells are so used to junk that they'll never quite get over it. They'll always crave dope. I'd never believed that before but I believed it now. Because even though I'd been clean for two years, and I knew there wasn't a trace of it left in my system, when I walked in that room it was like I had never left. My mouth was as dry as if I'd just swallowed cotton, and my nose started to run. I reached down and scratched my leg, which was suddenly itching like hell.

I didn't want it at all. It wasn't that. It was just those damn cells of mine. They wouldn't give up. They still thought they needed it.

But if my cells wanted dope, let them want it all day. They weren't getting any. I'd learned to ignore them. It wasn't exactly easy, but it got closer to easy all the time.

After a minute I looked at Paul. "No, thanks. That's not why I'm here." I took out the photo of Nadine Nelson and Jerry McFall. "You ever see her?"

Paul looked at the photo and smiled. "Sure, I know

her. Betty, right?" I shook my head. He frowned. "Well, I'm sure I know her. She's come by here. Ask Nell—she's in the front room with Jenny. Nell brought her around, I'm sure of it. And you know who the fellow is, right?"

"No," I said. "Who is he?"

"Jerry something," he said. He made a look on his face like he'd tasted something bad. "You don't know him? He's always been around."

"What's his story?" I asked.

Paul shrugged. "I don't know. Don't really know him. Just always struck me as a sleazy character, that's all."

That was like Einstein calling another man smart. I asked Paul if he had seen him lately and he said no, not for a few months.

The girl he just fixed crawled on her hands and knees over to a spot by the window where the sunlight was streaming in. Once she was in the sun, she curled up on the floor and dozed. I thanked Paul and went back to the two girls in the front room. They were in the same position they had been in before, but their eyes were open. I crouched down in front of them.

"Hi," I said. "I'm a friend of Paul's."

"Mmmmm," the girl with the black hair said. "Uh-huh." The blonde looked at the floor.

I showed them the photo. "I need to find this girl. Either of you know her? Paul said one of you brought her around here."

Slowly the girl with the black hair focused on the picture. "Hey," she said. "I think I know that girl."

"Good," I said. "Do you know where she is?"

"No, really," the girl said. "I think I know her. For real. She's a friend of Jenny's."

"Great. How does Jenny know her?"

"I dunno." She nudged her friend. "Hey, Jenny. Look. Who is that girl?"

Jenny slowly raised her head up to look at the photo. "Look," she said. "It's Jerry with that girl. What's-her-name." Her head fell back down and her eyes closed.

"You know him? Hey." I reached my hand up and took her by the chin. "Hey, wake up. You know him?"

Jenny opened her eyes and laughed. "Sure I do. Who the hell do you think got me started on this shit? He said he was gonna get me in pictures. . . ."

Her eyes were falling shut again. I grabbed her shoulder and shook her awake. "How about the girl, do you know her? Look." I put the photo in front of her face again. "This girl. Do you know her?"

"I think I used to work with her."

Her eyes shut and her head rolled back. She turned and snuggled up against her friend—I guess she was Nell. Nell kept her eyes open, but nothing was behind them. "Come on," I said to Nell. "You know where your friend works?"

She started to laugh. "She's a call girl, lady. She works everywhere."

That woke Jenny up. "I ain't no call girl," she muttered. "I'm a dancer."

"Oh yeah?" I asked. "Where do you dance?"

"I ain't no whore," she said. "I'm a dancer. Well, I used to be, but those bastards let me go on account of—"

"Come on," I said. "Where *were* you a dancer?"

"At Rose's. That's a nice place. I was a dancer at Rose's."


When I was on my way out I saw a man and a woman whispering together in the hallway on the ground floor. They were both skinny. The man wore an old suit with no hat or tie and the woman wore a black dress that had seen its best days ten years ago. They were probably plotting how to rip Paul off. People were always trying to rip Paul off. It never worked because no one could ever figure out where he kept his stash. It was in that big empty place somewhere but no one had ever figured out exactly where. It could drive you crazy. It drove me up the wall until I finally figured it out: in a glass jar under the floorboards in the bathroom.

The couple heard me coming down the stairs. The man nudged the woman and they stopped whispering. I was about to tell them not to worry, I wouldn't rat them out, when the woman looked up at me and I realized who it was. It took her a minute to recognize me and when she did she stared at me with a mean, sour look on her face.

I reached the bottom of the stairs and walked toward them.

"Josephine Flannigan," the woman said, with a voice to match her face. "What the hell are you doing here? If I find out you've been—"

I smiled. "Don't you worry, Cora. I'm just here to visit."

"Visit Paul?" she said sarcastically. "For the conversation? Give me a break, Joe."

"I swear it, Cora. Go up and ask him, if you like."

"Oh, I'll ask him," she said. "You can be sure of that. I'll ask every goddamned dope dealer in this town what you've been up to. And if I find out you've been using again, I'm gonna call the damn cops myself and have you locked up again."

"Come on," I said. "Take a good look. I'm clean, and I've been clean. And you ought to talk, lady."

She looked me up and down, saw that I was plump and that my hair was clean—that I didn't look anything like her—and decided I was telling the truth. "Okay," she finally said, her voice calmer now. "So come over here and give old Cora a kiss."

I did as she said. The man next to her ignored us both. "Jesus," I said. "If you're old, what does that make me?"

She smiled for the first time. "Ancient," she said, and laughed. "Anyway, don't talk about me. I'm hopeless. I'm hopeless and you know it."

She was right, so I didn't talk about her. "Figure out yet where Paul's keeping it?" I asked.

Cora stamped her foot and the man spat on the floor. "No, dammit," she said. "Joey, you must have an idea. Come on."

I shrugged. "Your guess is as good as mine."

Cora stamped her foot again. "Goddamn!" she said. "By the way, this is Hank. Hank, meet Joe. I've known Joe since I was young and pretty."

I laughed, but Cora didn't, because she wasn't kidding. She was my age, thirty-six, give or take a few years, but she hadn't aged well. She was too thin and her eyes were sunk deep in her head, with dark circles underneath. Deep lines framed her mouth and ran across her forehead.

Hank shook my hand. "So you're Josephine Flannigan," he said. "I've heard a lot about you."

I didn't know what he'd heard, so I didn't answer.

"Well," Cora said. "Seeing as how we're not having any luck with Paul, we better get to work somewhere else. Got any ideas, Joe?"

I thought for a minute. "Gimbel's isn't too bad around

this time," I said. "They've only got a few dicks working in the afternoons, none of them too bright. If you get there around one, it's pretty easy—all the secretaries are shopping, keeping the salesgirls tied up. If you can get to the jewelry counter, you can do pretty good."

Hank and Cora looked at each other, weighing their options.

"Just a few weeks back I got a nice little gold ring from Gimbel's," I added. "But don't even think about Macy's. The junkies burned it down, they're wise now. Got an undercover in every aisle. I won't even step foot in that place unless I've got my best suit on and my hair done."

Hank and Cora looked at each other again and nodded. Gimbel's it would be.

After they decided where to boost from, they started on where to buy from. "Frank's holding," Cora said.

Hank nodded. "Yeah. But there's too much sugar in his stuff. Ben's good, let's go see him."

"Ben?" Cora said, indignant. "I don't care how good it is, I'm not paying three dollars for one damn paper. Let's go to Jenny White."

"Jenny White?" Hank threw up his hands. "She beat me good last time."

"That wasn't her fault! No one had anything 'cause of all that shit in Mexico. Besides, Mick told me she's got some M . . ."

This sparked off a lively debate on exactly how much

M—morphine—was equal to how much H. Soon, I knew, they'd also have to bring in Dilaudid and opium into the comparison, even though no one was holding any, just to get all that squared away.

I stopped listening. A junkie could talk about junk from sunup to sundown. It was like a conversation that began when you took your first shot and didn't end until you'd had your last. Every junkie in New York, probably every addict in the world, could step into the conversation at any point and join in. There were a thousand and one topics, but they were all one topic: dope.

And there was so much to talk about. Every junkie was an investor who could discuss whether three dollars was better spent on three heavily cut papers from Mary or two pure syrettes from Joseph, a politician who knew how events in Europe and the Far East were affecting the distribution and pricing of drugs in New York, a lawyer who knew the letter of the drug laws in every state, and a psychiatrist who could tell you just the right way to hit up their dealer for one on the cuff.

But most of all, a junkie was a scientist. Everyone knew the business about your cells never being the same, of course. And everyone knew that dope addicts lived longer than anyone else, because dope preserved your cells, stopped them from aging—or they *would* live longer, if they didn't die from overdoses and liver failure and that type of thing. Speaking of liver failure, it was a known fact that it wasn't drugs that hurt your liver—it was the stuff the drugs were cut with. Pure dope wouldn't do you any harm at all, if it was all you shot. But pure dope could be dangerous if you weren't used to it. A junkie had to know exactly how much they could shoot of every form of opium there was, or risk shooting too much and overdosing.

I tried not to listen to Hank and Cora. I thought, This was why I quit. The never-ending conversation about dope, always the same loop, around and around. There was no aspect of junk that could go unexamined for more than twenty-four hours. I couldn't stand it anymore. A few minutes ago I had craved a shot like I was dying for one. And now more than anything else I hoped I would never have to speak to another junkie again. I liked Cora. I really did. I just wished there was something else she could talk about.

We had said goodbye and I was about to go when Cora pulled me close and whispered in my ear, "You wouldn't lie to me, would you, Joe?" she said. "Because I swear, if you're using again, after all you went through to get clean—"

"Yeah," I said. "I'd lie to you. But not about that."


When I left Cora and Hank I walked through the Lower East Side and went to Katz's on Ludlow Street for lunch.

Jim would have approved. I got my ticket and went up to the counter, where old Abe was cutting up a pastrami with a two-foot-long knife that would have scared the hell out of me if anyone else had been holding it.

"Joey," Abe said, smiling under his white hat. "Joey, you look good." I knew what he meant. What everyone meant when they said that. Not that my outfit was pretty or that my hair looked nice. They meant that I looked like I was off junk. It'd been two years now and I got a little tired of hearing it, but I guess I couldn't blame people for being surprised.

"Thanks, Abe. I feel good. How're the kids?"

"Real good," Abe said, slicing away with his knife. "The oldest, he's in college now. He's gonna be a doctor."

Right. He'd been saying the kid was going to be a doctor since the kid was knee high. He put my sandwich up on the counter and we talked some more. He told me the youngest was going to be a lawyer and the girl in the middle was going to marry a nice Jewish banker she'd met at temple. The fellow was all right but Abe was a little disappointed because he'd only gone to City College.

"You know how it is," he said. "He's a nice guy. But everyone wants the best for their kids, right? So I don't know why she couldn't find a fellow from Harvard." He shook his head. "At least NYU."

"Sure."

"Hey," Abe said, suddenly serious. "Did I tell you about Saul? Old Saul from Ludlow Street?"

I shook my head. I was sure I knew a Saul from somewhere, but . . .

"Sure," Abe said. "You know Saul. Old Saul on Ludlow Street. See, Saul, he was in the *schmata* business. Lived right here on Ludlow Street. Then he retires and he goes down to Florida. And every day he sits on the beach and he reads the anti-Semitic newspapers. You know the type. All about how the Jews are taking over the world."

"Sure," I said. I started to laugh already. It was a joke. "One pastrami shop at a time." I took another taste of corned beef.

But Abe kept it completely deadpan. "So Saul's reading the papers every day," he said. "Finally his wife, Sadie, she says, 'Saul. Saul,' she says. 'What are you reading this crap for?' And Saul smiles and he says, ''Cause I like to see how good we're doing. See, Sadie, right here, it says Jews control the banks, we own all the diamonds, we're running the government. . . . What more could we ask for?'"

I laughed so hard I almost spit out my corned beef.

"Sorry," Abe said to the man behind me. We'd been talking too long. "What can I get for you?"

I turned around and I got a start. I knew him, the man on line behind me. I couldn't place the face, but I was sure I'd seen him before. I got a strange feeling, like when Abe had first mentioned old Saul from Ludlow Street—I was supposed to know who it was, but . . .

Then I realized: it was the man who had been waiting across the street from Paul's. Guess he didn't have any luck finding his girl. I wasn't surprised. Once a girl spent a little time in Paul's, it was hard to get her out.

# Chapter Six

After lunch I took the subway up to Midtown and then walked a few blocks to Fifty-third between Broadway and Sixth. There in the middle of the block was a door between a theater and an office building with a sign painted on it: "ROSE's—Hi Class Lounge—COCKTAILS—Dancing—Right Upstairs!" The door opened up into a small, narrow staircase that reeked of booze and marijuana and cigarette smoke. The stairs took you into a room ten times the size you would have guessed—it was built on top of the theater next door.

In Rose's, taxi dancers would dance with a guy for a small fee; for a bigger fee they'd dance a little closer, although no one took their pants off and Tony, the manager, made sure everyone kept their hands where he could see them. It was a tough job, dancing in a dive like Rose's. But it paid okay and it beat the hell out of Woolworth's. It was close enough to Times Square to get the tourist trade and close enough to the better part of Midtown to get the local businessmen.

I worked there when I was hooked on dope. It was my husband who got me into it. Easy money, he said. Wear a low-cut dress with long sleeves to cover the track marks and the sores on your arms and they'll never know. You dance with a guy, spend some time with him, and then whatever happens after the club closes is your own business. Yours and your husband's. Except after a while, even with the long sleeves, they do know. And even the men who come to Rose's don't want to hang around a junkie. She might be good for one thing, but they're not going to pay her to dance and make conversation.

The place hadn't changed at all. Tony was right up at the cash register, like always, sitting on a stool, scowling over a pile of papers. Toward the left side of the room was a tiny stage where a three-piece band played "Blue Moon." It seemed like every joint in the world like Rose's played "Blue Moon," over and over again. The musicians looked like they were having trouble keeping their eyes open. There wasn't much else to the place; a dozen tables and two dozen chairs, a bar along the back wall, long red curtains keeping out the light, and a big open space for dancing. The lights were down almost low enough to make the girls look pretty and the men look handsome. Almost.

It was a slow day. There were more girls than customers, and only three couples were grinding away on the dance floor. The rest of the girls were up at the bar drinking cocktails.

"Joey!"

Tony stood up and came toward me with a smile. "Joey! Look at you! You look great, Joe, you really do."

"Thanks, Tony. How's everything around here?"

"Eh . . ." He had a list of complaints. The girls didn't look good, the guys were cheap, and the price of liquor was up. "So what brings you by," he finally asked. "Looking for a job?"

"Sure," I said, laughing. "How do you think I'd look in that?" I nodded my head toward a girl in a tight blue number I was around ten years too old for.

"Gorgeous," Tony said. And something about the way he said it choked me up a bit. But only for a second. I showed him the picture of Nadine and McFall.

"You ever see her in here?"

Tony took a good long look. "She looks like a girl who might have worked here for a couple of months. Not for long." He squinted at the picture. "Raquel?"

I shrugged. None of the girls at a spot like this used their real names.

Tony thought for a moment. "Raquel, I think. Maybe Roxanne? I don't know. The girls'll know, they'll remember. But honestly, Joe, I'm not even sure it's the same girl."

"How about the guy?"

Tony shrugged. "After a while, they all look alike."

I knew what he meant. I walked to the back, where the girls sat on stools by the bar. They were laughing and complaining over their half-price drinks, probably talking trash about Tony and the customers and the girls who were off that evening.

I recognized one of the girls, a brunette in a bright red dress, and I walked over to her. "Daisy," I said. She turned and looked at me. I could tell she didn't recognize me. The laughter quieted down. "I worked here for a while, maybe eight years back. I'm not surprised you don't remember me," I told her. "I spent most of my time in the first stall in the ladies' room."

That got a laugh from her and the rest of the girls. The first stall was bigger than the rest, and all the dope fiends preferred it for shooting. So now they knew I was telling the truth.

"Looking for work again?" Daisy asked, a bit friendlier now.

"No, actually, I'm looking for them."

I gave her the picture of McFall and Nadine. She looked at it and then back up at me. "Did she work here?"

"I don't know," I told her.

"She kinda looks familiar. . . . Gina, come here and look at this." A tall slim girl in a pink dress came down from the end of the bar. She looked at the photo over Daisy's shoulder.

"I don't know," Gina said, with a rough Brooklyn accent. "Isn't she the girl who left to go work at the Royale?"

"Maybe," Daisy said. "What was her name, anyway?"

Gina shrugged. "Jeez, they come and go so fast. Roxy?"

"Nah," Daisy said. "That ain't it. That was the girl who moved to Alaska."

A dark Puerto Rican girl leaned over and looked at the photo. "No," she said, with a Spanish accent. "That's the girl who went to the Royale. I went there once with a girlfriend—don't tell Tony, for Christ's sake—and I saw her there."

"When was that?" I asked.

She shrugged. "Over a month ago."

Gina pointed at McFall. "I dunno. But him, I think I've seen him before. Hey, Clara," she called. "Clara, come take a look." Clara was a pretty, curvy blonde in a fancy strapless white dress, like a girl might wear to a formal. She looked too young to be here. She hopped off her bar stool and came over to look. When she saw the photo she blinked and pursed her lips, just enough to see it if you were looking real close.

"No," she said quietly. I imagined that she always talked like that, quiet and soft. "I've never seen either one of them."

Daisy passed the photo down the bar. The rest of the girls said they hadn't seen either of them. I thanked them, and they went back to their drinks and their chatter. Except Clara, the blonde. She sat on her stool and looked at the floor.

"Hey," I said to her, smiling. "Let's have a drink."

She nodded. I took her by the arm and led her over to a table a few yards away from the bar, where we sat across from each other. She didn't resist. Her arm was soft and practically limp and it sort of made you feel like crying to touch her.

"How do you know him?" I asked.

She shrugged, defeated. Her pretty face looked young and tired. She looked down at the floor again. "We went out to dinner a few times, that was all."

"You meet him here?"

She nodded. "Yeah. We went out to dinner a few times, that was all."

But that wasn't all. She was still looking down at the floor. "Why'd you only go out a few times?"

"That guy," she said, sighing. "He seemed different, you know? Nice. He really seemed like *somebody*."

"And then?"

She kept her eyes down at the floor.

"Did you go to bed with him?" I prodded.

She looked up. "Yeah, I did. And when I woke up in the morning, all my money was gone. Two hundred and twenty-five dollars. I was saving it in a little tin on my dresser."

"You ever see him again?"

She shook her head, relaxing back into a slouch, her eyes turning back toward the floor. "Boy. It took me a long time to save up that two hundred and twenty-five dollars."

I talked with Tony for a while before I left. When I was getting ready to go a group of five businessmen came in. They were fat, with shiny pink faces, and they were laughing like going to spend money on taxi dancers was the funniest thing they had ever done. Like that's why they were doing it—for laughs. When the girls by the bar saw them come in they pulled themselves up a little straighter and stopped making jokes and put on demure, hopeful smiles. Like they were just waiting for the right fat businessman with the right red face in the right cheap suit to come and save them.

On my way out I saw that Clara was still sitting at the table where I left her, alone, looking down at the floor.

# Chapter Seven

I slept late the next day because I could. If I was going to the Royale there was no point in going before the sun went down. I'd thought I'd heard something about April showers bringing May flowers but it must have just been a rumor, because here we were in May and it was pouring like hell. It was raining when I woke up and still raining after I cleaned up my room and picked up my wash and put away my clothes and went shopping for new stockings and gloves and got ready to go out.

Late in the afternoon I took the subway up to Times Square, where I went to the Automat for lunch. I'd grown up just outside the Square, in Hell's Kitchen, and coming down to the Automat was a big treat. It was always loud and busy and full of regular working people—stiffs, my mother called them. People with regular jobs, people who owned houses, or at least I imagined they did. In Hell's

Kitchen we'd moved from one tenement or rooming house to another every few months. My mother would get us kicked out for one reason or another—too many parties, too much noise, too many men coming and going all night, and of course the rent was always late. I couldn't remember half of the rooms we'd lived in, which was probably for the best. Sometimes I'd walk by a run-down building on Fifty-fifth Street and think it looked familiar, but I was never really sure.

In the Automat you'd put a nickel or a dime in a machine and open a little glass door and get a sandwich or a dish of macaroni with cheese or a piece of cherry pie. I never knew until I was older that there were ladies working behind the machines, putting the food in. When I was a kid I'd come and get a Coke. I could never afford anything good, and it's hard to steal from the Automat—you could do it if you caught the door just after someone had gotten their dish and you reached far back, but then a man would come over and kick you out. Those ladies saw everything, I guess. When I got older I learned that if you hung around with a cup of coffee and looked hungry a man would always come along to buy you something. The trick then was to leave before the man wanted payback for the nickel he'd spent on pie.

But now I had plenty of dough, and I had two pieces of pie without having to look over my shoulder. When I left the Automat it had stopped raining and I walked around for a while. Times Square was full of tourists looking up at the lights. Maybe they didn't have electricity back at home. On the corner of Forty-second and Seventh a group of queer boys hung around in tight dungarees, waiting for tricks, insulting each other and laughing at their own jokes and trying to pass the time. In front of the dime museum on Forty-second Street a barker in a coat and tails with a turban on his head tried to talk the people passing by into seeing Professor Thaddeus's Educated Fleas. I declined. I'd seen them before and they weren't all that educated. A group of sailors in navy whites stood around and watched the barker, wondering over it all, and an old man in a trench coat, worn at the cuffs, was watching along with the sailors. The old man's face hung down with age, and a few gray hairs were left under the rim of his hat. Under the trench coat he wore a suit that had been pretty sharp ten years ago, when he'd bought it, but now it was faded and shiny from being cleaned too many times. The old man kept his eyes on the barker, but slowly, one step at a time, he was moving closer to one of the sailors.

The old man was just getting ready to relieve the sailor closest to him of his wallet when the barker spotted him. The barker opened his mouth to say something when I stepped in and took the old man by the arm. "Grandpa!"

I said, loudly. "I've told you a thousand times, I don't want you spending your relief check on the naked girls in the dime museum!"

The old man was Yonah Ross, probably the oldest living junkie in New York—he wasn't all that old but it was still a pretty big accomplishment. Part of it was due to the fact that he never sold it, like most do at one time or another, so no one ever had a beef with him. Instead he stuck to street cons, from pickpocketing and shoplifting to three-card monte, selling fake opium to tourists and leading sailors to fake hookers. He had lived with my mother for a while when I was a girl. A lot of men had lived with my mother but Yonah was different. He liked kids and he taught me a lot.

The sailors looked at each other and decided that naked girls *and* educated fleas were worth a dime. They went inside. The barker took their money and then turned around to hiss at Yonah. "You're lucky she showed up," he said, "or I'd have the coppers here. Now beat it, and don't come back."

Yonah looked glum as we walked away. "Jesus," he said, after he thanked me for getting him out of there. "That son-of-a-bitch carney. Who's he think he is? You know I knew his old man, and him, he never gave me a hard time. I used to steer guys to the museum and they let me have the crowds out front. We used to work together back then, everyone in the Square. The hookers would let me know who had the rolls and I'd let them know who I'd already gotten to, so we wouldn't all be wasting our time. Now it's every man out for himself. It's a dog-eat-dog world out here." He shook his head at the immorality of it all. We walked past Howard Johnson's. Yonah had his eye on a couple of out-of-town businessmen standing in front, but I walked him past them. He smiled at me. "Jesus, Joey, you look great, just great. How you feeling these days? You doin' good?"

"Great," I said. "I'm doing great. But listen, Yonah, let me buy you a drink. Maybe you can help me with something."

"Sure, doll, sure. But I gotta go back to my room for a bit just now. You want to come?"

I went along with him to his room on Forty-second and Ninth. We talked about the good old days on the way there. All the fun times we had when he taught me how to grind up oregano so it looked like weed, and you could sell it to suckers for a dollar or more. Those grand old times when he sat me down and explained to me what a badger was, and introduced me to a man who would pull it off with me—I'd pretend to be a hooker and the man would pretend to be my angry father. I'd find a trick and just before we did the deed Pa would bust in, and the trick would give Pa all the cash he had on him to stop him from calling the cops. Yonah had meant well, though, and I'd probably be a lot worse off now if I had never met him. You needed something to fall back on in this life.

He lived in a hotel called the Prince Alexander. It seemed like half the fleabag hotels in the world were called the Prince Something-or-Other. And all of them used to be nice. When you walked into the Prince Alexander there were marble floors covered in enough filth not to need rugs, and a wooden desk for registration that was wrapped up in a chicken wire cage. That was something you could count on in any Prince hotel. The desk would be wrapped in chicken wire.

Behind the desk was a skinny young guy reading a girlie magazine. He nodded at Yonah when we came in. In the lobby a group of men around Yonah's age, drunks and nutcases, hung around watching life go by, or at least the slice of it that came through the Prince Alexander. We stopped to say hello. I knew some of them: One-Eyed Fred and Fifty-third Street Jackson and Nuthouse Jim. It was hard to believe it now but once they'd really been something, the old men in the Prince Alexander—con men and hustlers and stick-up men. When I was a kid we all wanted to be just like them when we grew up. And now it was looking more and more like I would be.

Off to the side sat an old gent wearing a brown suit and a white shirt with a high collar and a bowler hat that looked like it was from 1915. He was tall and thin and sat perfectly straight, talking to himself softly without stopping. From what I heard it was about a woman named Emily.

"Emily said she would be home in five minutes but it wasn't five minutes it was six, six and a half, a half dozen doughnuts . . ."

Yonah led me through the lobby to the elevator, which he ran himself to take us up to the third floor. At the end of a long hallway lined with peeling wallpaper and dim bare-bulb lights and locked doors was Yonah's room. It pretty much made my room at the Sweedmore look like a suite at the Plaza. There was just enough room for a single bed—a cot, really—and an old green chair with the stuffing poking out. The cot had dirty grayish sheets on it, tangled up with each other in a knot. Clothing hung from nails on the wall.

"Sit, doll." Yonah smiled and took off his hat and coat and put them on the bed. I sat on the chair. The room smelled awful. On the floor was an overflowing ashtray. "I'll be right back," he said.

Yonah left the room to get his works and his dope, probably hidden in the hall somewhere. It was safer there. If the cops tossed his room it'd be clean, and if anyone found his stuff in the hall they couldn't prove it was his. I looked around. A yellowed sheet was hung over the window but it sagged on one side, and I could see that the sun had come out just in time for it to go down, turning the sky yellow and gray. A minute later

Yonah came back with his kit, wrapped in a dirty white handkerchief, in his hand.

"Excuse me for a minute, Josephine," he said. He sat down at the head of the bed, facing the door. His back was to me but I could hear everything he was doing. First he took off his right shoe and let it drop to the ground, and then his sock. Then he measured a little junk from a paper envelope into a spoon. Next he used his works to suck up a few drops of water from a glass I guessed he kept under the bed and squirted it into the spoon. Then he lit a match and heated up the mixture in the spoon until it was a good smooth gold-colored liquid. Finally he pulled the whole mixture up into his works through a little piece of cotton. Then he poked around for a while, cursing a few times as he looked for a good vein. "Ah, all right, here we go," he said as he found a good one. Then he injected into a vein in his foot. The veins in his arms were probably gone twenty years ago, collapsed from overuse. He was lucky to still have his feet left—for most of the old-timers it was the crotch or the neck.

He sat quietly for a minute. It wasn't that being high felt so good, especially not when you'd been shooting as long as Yonah had. You could hardly even call it being high. It was that nothing else felt bad. There were no aches, no pains, no memories, no shame. Nothing mattered now. It was like junk took you up just a few feet above everybody else, just enough so you didn't have to involve yourself in all the petty problems of the world. Those weren't your problems anymore. Let someone else worry. You could watch it all and feel nothing. For that little piece of time you had everything you needed, everything you had ever wanted.

He put his sock and shoe back on and turned around to face me, swinging his legs over to the side of the bed.

"Jesus, Joe, are you okay?"

I realized I had been holding my breath. My jaw was clenched so tight it hurt to let it go. I took a deep breath.

"Yeah, I'm fine, thanks." Yonah hadn't taken a big shot, just enough to maintain, and so he was good for a couple of questions. I showed him the picture of Nadine Nelson and Jerry McFall and asked if he knew them.

Yonah thought for a moment, nodding his head. Then he got a look on his face, like he had just tasted a quart of milk and found out that it had spoiled. "Yeah. Him I know. Her, no, I don't think so—maybe I seen her, but I ain't sure. But him, I know who he is. Jerry McFall."

"What's he all about?"

Yonah shifted position on the bed, making himself comfortable. He sighed with contentment. "He's an asshole. A pimp."

I had guessed as much, but I hadn't been sure. I didn't know exactly where Nadine was now, but at least I knew what she was doing. "Does he use?" I asked.

Yonah nodded. "Yeah, he's been a junkie for years. But he's a real swell, you know," he said sarcastically. "Goes out on the town, hangs out with all the punk hustlers trying to make good. Wears fancy suits, makes like a real big shot. Says he's in pictures." Yonah laughed. "Sometimes he takes pictures of the girls to sell to magazines. You know what I mean. But how the guy makes a living is, he's got girls working for him. All on dope. And he sells, too. Not much. Just to the girls mostly, the girls he's got working for him. You know how it is. He's gotta take care of 'em or they'd find someone else."

"Does he sell good stuff?" I asked.

Yonah shrugged. "I don't know. I don't buy from him. He's got a whole crowd, young folks, I don't really mix with them."

"Seen him around lately?" I asked Yonah.

"I ain't seen him," Yonah said. "But I'll keep my eyes open. What do you want with a punk like that, anyways?"

"Not much," I said. "Someone just asked me to find him, that's all."

"Eh," Yonah said. "It won't be too hard. Guys like that, they're always out and about, painting the town red." He closed his eyes for a minute. I looked down at the floor. There was a newspaper, two weeks old, open to an advertisement for a ladies' dress shop.

I picked it up. Yonah heard the paper rustle and

opened his eyes. He smiled. "Hey, did you see? That's Shelley, in the paper. You can have it if you want."

"No," I started. "That's not—" But then I looked again. He was right, it was Shelley. I hadn't recognized her. She was wearing a black dress that was tight at the waist and full on the bottom. Just two little straps held it up on top. Her hair was combed so smooth it shone, done up in a big *thing* on the top of her head, and she had on more makeup than a hooker, although somehow it didn't look whorish at all. Under the picture was printed: *Just in time for spring!*

In the photo with the jewelry she had looked pretty enough, but I had recognized her right away. Here, though, she looked like some kind of movie star, the way they did her hair and makeup. Like a girl who had money. A girl who'd been all over the world. A girl who could get whatever she wanted just by snapping her fingers, who was used to the best of everything, who'd never had to beg, borrow, or steal a damn thing in her life.

Of course, she had always kind of looked like that. Shelley had never been like the rest of us. Like how most girls in our neighborhood never wore a new dress, just hand-me-downs from their mothers and sisters. Shelley wouldn't go to school in an old dress. If I wanted her to go to school I had to take her to Mabel's Ladies' Wear and buy her a new dress every September. But it had always been like playacting before. She could wear all the new dresses she wanted, but she was still Shelley. It was still the same girl, who didn't go to a better school or have a better mother or a better home than the rest of us. If she wanted a piece of pie from the Automat she didn't have a nickel to buy one unless I gave it to her, because I wouldn't let her hang around there and wait for a man to come along. I didn't want her to think it was all right for her to hang around and wait for a man to buy her something she should have been able to buy herself.

But when I looked at her now, it was like she really was someone else. Like she had never lived in Hell's Kitchen at all. She was about as far away from the Prince Alexander hotel as you could get.

Something about seeing Shelley like that spooked me. "Thanks," I said. I folded the paper up, careful not to crease the picture, and put it in my purse.

"Maybe she knows this McFall." Yonah shrugged. "She's young, she knows that whole crowd." His eyes slowly fell closed again.

I frowned. "Why? You've seen her lately?" I liked Yonah. In a way, you could say I loved him. But that didn't mean I wanted Shelley hanging around him.

"I don't know, doll," he answered, leaning back against the wall. "When you're old, sometimes you just don't know anymore—I mean, you see someone last year and it seems like last week." He sighed. "Nothing's the same anymore. In those days it was money for nothing. I tell you, doll, I didn't know how good we had it. Now it's always a hassle, hassle from the cops, from the squares, even the other fellows on the deuce. It's like a person don't even have the right to exist anymore, just 'cause he likes a taste of dope once in a while." He shook his head. "Hey, remember when we used to go out and get cab fare together?"

"Sure." Yonah would dress up like a businessman and I'd be his daughter. We'd go to Grand Central Station and pretend like his wallet had been lifted. All the other businessmen would give us cab fare to get home.

Yonah smiled. "Was your mother mad when we got home."

"She took the money just the same," I said. She hadn't been mad because of what we did. It was because we went without her, and she was scared we'd hold out on her.

He laughed, coughing a little. "Yeah, she sure did. She was something, wasn't she? I know she wasn't much of a mother, but she was a hell of a lot of fun. And Shelley, too. She was pissed as hell, you going out without her. You never let that girl do nothin'. But you always took good care of them. You always took care of them good. Your mother, money used to go through her hands like water. . . ."

His voice trailed off and he started to doze. I stared

for a while at his works, lying on the floor next to him. Next to the needle and syringe was a little cloth pouch. I was sure the dope was in there. He'd have a nice amount, with his habit. He wouldn't even miss a little taste. He wouldn't even know it was gone.

I looked at it for a while. Then I quietly got up, took a twenty-dollar bill from my purse, and put it in the little pouch. I lay Yonah down on the bed and left, shutting the door behind me.

# Chapter Eight

The Royale was on Forty-seventh Street off of Ninth Avenue. It used to be a real theater, and the outside still had the old plaster decoration, mermaids and Egyptians and waves, a whole hodgepodge that maybe somehow made sense together back in the twenties, when the place was built. But instead of the name of a show, the marquis said: *Girls! Girls! Girls! Live Revue Inside!* You walked into the lobby and the first thing you saw, just like the sign said, was girls. The dancers stood around the lobby in between their acts to lure the fellows inside. They stood up straight and flashed big smiles and wore shiny lipstick, but they weren't pretty. It was a hard life, and it aged you fast. They still wore their stage dresses, spangly evening gowns rigged up to come off easy, and in the light you could see that they were stained, and half the sequins had fallen off. They smoked cigarettes and tried to look cheerful, enforced by a guy in a cheap tux about two inches shorter than me. Two of the girls whispered to each other about a third.

"She's such a bitch."

"I know. Over a goddamned hairpin, can you believe it?"

"She's always been like that. She's a whore. You can't let it get to you. . . ."

When I tried to walk through the door into the theater the cheap tux stopped me. "Sorry," he said, with a good long leer. "No single ladies allowed."

That was standard in these joints, to keep out the streetwalkers. They didn't want the competition.

"I'm here on business," I told him. "Business with the management."

He looked me up and down. "They ain't hiring."

"Gee, now you've hurt my feelings," I said, "but it ain't that kind of business."

"Well then, what kind of business?"

"The kind that's none of your business at all."

He tried another angle. "You know there's a two-drink minimum. That's one for you and one for a girl."

"Two whole drinks?" I asked. "I think I can handle it."

"I don't know," he said. "The drinks in there ain't cheap. And I got word from the boss—no single ladies inside. Not unless . . ."

I took a dollar out of my purse and handed it to him. He took the dollar and looked at it real close before he crumpled it up and put it in his pocket.

"You know," I told him, "a gypsy once told me that it was bad luck, to crumple your money up like that."

"Yeah, like I need advice from you," he said, stepping aside to let me in. But he did take the bill back out of his pocket and smooth it out between his fingers before he put it away again.

Inside the lights were dim and had a red tint. The big stage had been left in place and a woman stood up there now doing something like a shimmy in a white dress. You wouldn't exactly call it dancing. Behind her, a band that looked barely alive finished up their daily dose of "Blue Moon" and began "Stardust." On the floor, the rows of seats had been torn out and replaced by tables and chairs. A few men sat near the stage and watched, as if there was really a show going on. But at most of the tables there were girls, sitting alone or with men or with each other. That was the real attraction. They'd spend a few minutes each day on stage and the rest hustling guys for drinks and whatever else they could get out of them.

Nadine had been going pretty quickly downhill. From Rose's to here. Next was just good old-fashioned turning tricks on the streets.

A woman stepped out from behind the bar and headed my way. She was a tall brunette around my age with a hard face, wearing a tight black suit. Before she had a chance to give me the same routine as the doorman I showed her the photo of Nadine and McFall. She looked at me for a long time before she looked at the photo, and then she only glanced at it.

"I don't know," she said. "That could be anyone." I asked if it was all right if I spoke to some of the girls. She looked at me and shrugged. "You wanna buy a girl a drink, you can do whatever you want with her."

I figured the Nelsons had given me enough dough to shell out a little. I went over to a table full of girls without men by the stage.

"Hi," I said. "I'm Josephine. And I'd like to buy you all a drink."

They looked at each other and giggled, and then they all made space for me at the table. A waitress came by and took their orders: one Tom Collins, one sloe gin fizz, a pink lady, a mimosa, a whiskey sour, a ginger ale for the lady picking up the tab, and a bourbon, on the rocks. The bourbon was a dark-haired girl in a black dress who looked like she'd already had a few today, and plenty the day before.

The girls tittered excitedly and whispered to each other until their drinks came. Anything unusual in a place like this, like a lady buying drinks, was cause for excitement. It could get pretty dull on an ordinary day. When they were settled in with their cocktails I passed around the photo of Nadine and McFall.

"Oh sure, she used to work here," one girl said, a blonde in a pink dress with lipstick to match. "And him, he's around here all the time. What's her name, Trixie?"

"No," the next girl said, a chubby redhead in green. "Trixie was that other girl, the one who went to Alaska. This is Belle. You remember." She handed the photo to a girl across the table who looked about sixteen. The jailbait looked at the photo and shrugged. "Belle? Maybe. But I thought her name was Candy."

"Nah," the bourbon said, with a low, raspy alcoholic's voice. She was looking at the photo over the jailbait's shoulder. "She was one of McFall's girls. The guy in the picture. One of those goddamned junkies. Ask what's-her-name." She nodded toward a little brunette who looked twenty years old, sitting alone at a table in the corner. I hadn't noticed her before. She was thin and wore a black dress with long sleeves to cover her track marks. Her face was hollow where there should have been flesh, and even though she was still pretty she also looked like she was dying. "She works for that rat bastard, too. She knows her, I'm sure of it."

"Why's he a rat bastard?" I asked.

She scowled. "Junkies, all of them. He gets those girls hooked on dope and then gets 'em working here.

Some of 'em are just kids, you know. Anyway, ask any girl here, they'll have a story about Jerry McFall. All of us who are independent, like me, who work for ourselves, he's always trying to recruit us. Like I want to give half my money to some rat bastard so he can hook kids on dope. Junkies," she said. "They're the worst."

Right, I thought. Except for alcoholics.

I thanked the girls and left money on the table for another round of drinks before I went over to the little brunette. She smiled at me.

"Hi," I said. "Can I buy you a drink?"

"Sure," she said, with a sweet young voice. I sat down next to her.

"What's your name?" she asked.

"Josephine," I said. She kept her eyes on me like it was the most fascinating word anyone had ever spoken. I realized what was going on—she thought I was a customer.

"Actually," I said, "I'm hoping you can help me with something. I'm looking for a girl, and you might know her."

Her smile faded somewhat. No lesbian meal ticket for her tonight. But I'd paid for a drink and she could only get it down so fast, and until it was done she was stuck with me. She nodded when I showed her Nadine's picture. "Sure," she said. "Nanette. I know her. "

I couldn't believe it. Here was someone who actually knew Nadine. Not just remembered maybe seeing her once, but really knew her. I felt like a fifty-pound weight had come off my shoulders.

"Good," I said. "Do you know where she is?"

The girl looked around, trying to find a better prospect for the evening. "Listen," I said seriously, trying to get her attention. "This girl has a family, and they care about her. They want to take her home, and they don't care if she's on drugs. I've met them myself, and they're good people. She'd be a lot better off than she is here, don't you think?"

Something caught the girl's eye across the room. I turned and looked. A middle-aged man was sitting alone near the stage, smiling at her. He waved at her. She waved back with a big smile. I could see that my little speech had had a profound effect on her.

"He's a regular," she said. "I really should—"

I reached into my purse and pulled out a five-dollar bill and gave it to her. She reached out for it but I held it back. "Listen," I said. "For five dollars, I want answers. Are you gonna give them to me?"

"Sure," she said, offended. "I'm just trying to make a living here."

I held out the bill and she snatched it up and stuffed it in her shoe before I could blink.

"So where is she?" I asked.

"I don't know where she is," the girl said. "The last time I talked to her was, I don't know, four or five days ago." She looked over her shoulder and held up her hand to her trick, telling him she'd just be a minute.

"Tell me the whole story, from the beginning," I said. I could already feel the fifty pounds settle back on my shoulders. "From when you first met Nanette."

She nodded her head and reached down to scratch her leg. "Okay. Nadine—that's her real name—Nadine started coming around here a month ago, maybe two months. She'd never, well, you know, been in a place like this before. So Jerry—he's a friend of ours." Working girls never called their pimps *pimps*. It was always just a nice guy out to give them a helping hand. "He asked me to look out for her, and I did. Real nice girl, but kind of dumb. Jerry set us up in the same hotel. She was always drawing pictures when she wasn't working." She smirked, like drawing pictures proved Nadine was dumb. "Then about a week ago, her and Jerry, they take off for a few days. I talked to the other girls, no one knew where they were. That wasn't so strange—sometimes Jerry takes a girl on a little vacation like that, if she's doing really well or if maybe she needs a talking-to. But anyway, one night I go back to the hotel and Nadine's waiting outside the hotel, crying. No one would let her in 'cause Jerry hadn't paid her bill. He hadn't paid mine, either, but I took care of it myself, from what I made. So I snuck her in through the back door—like I said, she was kind of dumb, 'cause she could have done that herself—and we jimmied the lock to her room, so she could get her stuff."

She smiled at the man across the room again.

"So what happened?" I asked.

"Well, according to Nadine, Jerry tells Nadine they're going out on a date, right? So he takes her to this apartment—"

"Where?" I asked.

"She didn't say. So he takes her to this apartment, and no one's there. So of course Nadine, it took her a long time to realize they were robbing someone. Nadine said she was so nervous she almost started to cry!" That made the girl laugh. "So Jerry tells her to watch the door and holler if she sees someone coming." Right. So Jerry could slip out a back window and Nadine would be left to take the heat.

"But they got caught?" I asked.

The girl nodded. "Jerry had his car downstairs. I guess he found what he was looking for, 'cause after a few minutes they split and they go down to the car. But then another car pulls in behind them, just as they're taking off. When that happens, well, Jerry just about loses his mind—Nadine said he turned white as a ghost!" This also made her laugh. Nothing like the misery of others for a good joke. "So Nadine figures they were busted pretty good. That whoever was in the car behind them, well, that's whose apartment it was. 'Cause the other car, they turned on the lights and made sure they got a real good look at who it was. They didn't try to chase 'em or nothin'—just let Jerry and Nadine know they'd seen 'em."

"Huh," I said. "So where's Nadine now?"

"I dunno," she said.

I sighed. "Well, where'd she go when she left your hotel?"

"I dunno," the girl said again. "She said she was gonna meet Jerry somewhere, and they'd be laying low for a few days until everything cooled down. But I ain't seen either of them since."

"So what did they steal?" I asked.

She smiled. "Dope, Nadine figured. 'Cause Jerry had been running dry before and afterwards he was rolling in it. She gave me some, too."

"Do you have any idea where Jerry usually got his stuff from?" I asked.

The girl shook her head. "Uh-uh. I know he hated the guy, though. I heard Jerry moaning about him a couple of times." She laughed. "Guess the guy thought he was really someone, thought he was better than Jerry. It really burned him up."

So Jerry got Nadine involved in ripping off a dope dealer and now they were both in trouble. Great.

That was all the girl knew. She finished her drink and

was about to meet the man across the room when I stopped her.

"So you've just been coming here to work every night," I asked, "even though Jerry hasn't been around in a week?" It wasn't any of my business, but I was curious.

"Oh, I've got a new fellow now," she said quickly. "Arnie. He started coming around a few days after Jerry split. He takes real good care of me. Of all the girls. We're lucky he came around when he did." She hugged herself, and her big brown eyes widened. "You wouldn't want to be out here all by yourself."

# Chapter Nine

This was what I knew so far: Nadine had met McFall while she was at Barnard. After she got kicked out she stayed with him. I could imagine how it played out. He said things like *Don't worry, baby, I'll always take care of you. You'll never have to worry about a thing.* He sent her to work at Rose's, or maybe it was her own decision. But the money she made there wasn't enough to feed her habit and leave a slice for McFall, so she moved—or he moved her—to the Royale, where it was easier to pick up dates. *Of course I don't want to see you with other men, baby. It kills me. But how else are we gonna pay the bills?* He sent her to live at the hotel the girl had mentioned. Now that he had her turned out, why keep her around to cramp his style? *It's just temporary. Just until we have enough saved up to get our own place, out in the country somewhere. None of these other girls mean anything—it's just so I can make more money for the two of us. You know that.*

Then McFall got the clever idea to rip off his dope connection. The connection could have been just about anyone in the five boroughs of New York. Dope came into town through the mob, but by the time it got down to the level of Jerry McFall, probably ten men had bought it, stepped on it, and passed it along. McFall's connection was probably someone who never sold on the street, probably someone who didn't use. A businessman, so to speak. But certainly not a real player, and not a mob man himself. The junkies who actually sold it to other users were the bottom of the barrel and they made the smallest profit, because no one higher up in the barrel would deal with them. All I knew about the man was that it was someone Jerry didn't like. That didn't help me at all. From what I knew, Jerry didn't like anyone too much.

But the job went wrong, and now Jerry and Nadine were hiding out somewhere. Probably somewhere in New York City, but maybe not. Maybe they were shacked up at Jerry's aunt's barn in Idaho.

I was ready to give up on the whole damn thing. There wasn't really any reason for me to find her. The first thousand was already mine and the second—well, even if I did find Nadine, who knew if the Nelsons would pony up? I didn't have any reason to think they would, especially once they saw her. If they thought they were getting the old Nadine back, they were in for a shock. They were looking for a college girl whose biggest problem had been that she didn't fit in at the country club in Westchester. From what I'd heard so far, if I brought them anything at all it would be an addict who'd been with more men than the rest of the country club combined. They probably wouldn't even want her in the house. And I couldn't exactly take them to court if they decided to renege.

I'd be better off going back to my regular work, going back to lifting wallets and hitting the department stores. Maybe even use the thousand bucks to get a bigger con going. Buy some new clothes, set something up for myself. Or I could use the money to take a vacation. I had a girlfriend in Florida I could stay with for a week. There was an old boyfriend in New Orleans I could visit. I'd never been to New Orleans.

I had plenty of problems of my own, and the more I started looking at it, the more it looked like this wasn't going to be so easy after all. The girl wasn't just missing as far as her parents were concerned, like I had thought. She was missing, period. Even Nadine's friends, or the closest she had to them, didn't know where she was. The trail ended at the Royale, just where it would be hardest to pick it up. There were only about ten thousand girls selling it at any given moment in New York. It would be like looking for a piece of hay in a haystack. The cops might know something but it wasn't likely, and even if they did, there was no way any cop was helping me.

I was at a dead end. And if she was in trouble now, it was her own fault. Her whole life, when you looked at it, was one lucky break after another. The girl had had everything handed to her on a silver platter. Never had any worries over money, more than good-looking enough, and from what everyone said she had a real talent, too, with the whole art thing. Her parents cared about her more than most parents cared about their kids. My own mother had been pleased as punch when I left home, and I was a lot younger than Nadine. I was always spoiling her fun, worrying about food and clothes and boring stuff like that, and she sure didn't hire some private dick to track me down. When she died we hadn't spoken in ten years.

This girl was going to college, for Christ's sake. I'd never known anyone who'd been to college. I wasn't even sure what they did there. I left school in the ninth grade. I knew why my life had turned out the way it did—I'd never had much to lose to begin with. And I'd never been good at anything that was legal. But this girl, she'd thrown away what ninety percent of the world would kill for. I didn't care if her parents did spank her or her mother did tip the bottle a little. She'd had no reason to do it. She'd had no right to do it.

Besides, I figured that soon enough she'd go home on

her own anyway. The first time a trick got rough with her or another girl pulled her hair, she'd go back home crying to Westchester and her parents would send her to get a cure somewhere. She'd get all the best doctors and all the best drugs and she'd pick up her life just where she'd left off. She'd marry one of the boys from the country club in a white dress, and everyone would forget all about her little episode in the city.

So there was no reason for me to go any further with it. There was no reason for me to keep looking for the girl at all. I didn't owe her a damn thing.

To hell with it. I was through.

Before I left the Royale I went to the ladies' room. There was a lounge inside, with pink wallpaper peeling off the walls. The Royale used to be a nice theater once, about a thousand years before. There was one wall of private stalls, one of sinks, and a third done up with vanity tables and chairs and a long mirror. Two girls were sitting at the mirror, laughing and putting on makeup. They were in their late twenties, with figures that looked younger and eyes that looked older, wearing tight dresses and too much makeup. One had a henna rinse in her hair, the other bleach.

I took a seat next to them and took out a compact. One of them, the blonde, smiled at me. On impulse I took out the photo and handed it to her.

"If you don't mind," I said, "do either of you know them?"

She took the photo and looked. Her girlfriend did the same. Then they looked at each other. They weren't smiling anymore.

"I'm Joey," I said.

"Miriam," said the redhead. The blonde said, "Hazel."

Their eyes met in the mirror. Miriam nudged Hazel with her knee.

"You might as well tell her," Miriam said. "Imagine how you'd feel if the same thing happened to her."

"What's that?" I asked quickly, before Hazel had a chance to change her mind.

"Well," she began, with a shaking voice. She looked down at her makeup and back up at the mirror. She tried a smile. "I mean . . . let's just say . . ."

She gave up and looked back down at her makeup again. She wanted to tell me. She just couldn't.

I turned around to face her. "What did he do?"

Hazel didn't say anything, just looked at her makeup like it was the most important thing in the world. But Miriam answered. "I'll tell you what he did. First, he took her out a couple of times. Dinner, dancing, you know—"

"Oh, Miriam," Hazel said, trying to stop her as if she were making a big deal out of nothing.

But it didn't work. "And then he goes to pick her up at her house—"

"Miriam, really."

"—and the bastard tries to get fresh, you know?"

"Sure," I said.

Miriam snorted. "And listen, she's no virgin, neither am I, and I bet you ain't either—"

"That's for sure."

"But you know, she hardly knew the guy, and she didn't even like him that much, and he wasn't paying for it. So when she says no, let's just go out, he starts slapping her around, like he owns her or something. She had a black eye for days, couldn't even leave the house! And then—"

Hazel powdered her face. "Miriam, really. Come on."

"And then he made her anyway?" I guessed.

"Yeah, that's what he did," Miriam spat out. "He made her do it anyway. With a black eye, and her lip was bleeding and everything. I mean, we've all had rough dates before. But this was different, this guy, he was supposed to be . . ." She looked for the right phrase. "One of us."

"How long ago was that?" I asked.

"A couple of months, maybe?" Miriam guessed.

Hazel looked up. Tears were running down her cheeks, leaving sharp tracks of real skin through her makeup. "Yeah," she said. "Maybe two months." She turned back to the mirror and began putting on lipstick. Me and

Miriam did the same. The show was over, and we were back to strangers again.

"So you watch yourself," said Miriam. "You be careful with that one."

I thanked her, and said I would be.

I knew Nadine was only getting what she'd asked for. She wanted her walk on the wild side and now she was getting it. So let her see what The Life was like. Let her lose her looks from getting hit in the face too many times. Let her lose a few teeth and all of her pride and all her charm school manners. Her college education wouldn't do her any good out here. And if she thought that drawing some pretty pictures would keep away a cop looking for a freebie, let her try. That pretty face would only make the girls hate her more and the men want to hurt her worse.

She was no better than me or anyone else. So why shouldn't she? Why the hell shouldn't she?

There was no reason at all for me to keep looking for Nadine Nelson. But I did.

# Chapter Ten

When I got home Lavinia had a message for me from Jim: if I wanted to see him, he'd be at Mr. Chan's in Chinatown around nine. I got there at quarter after. Jim was sitting at a booth with Mr. Chan, giving him stock tips. Chan's restaurant had been there since before I could remember, probably since before I was born, and he knew just about everyone in New York. He must have been older than the hills, but didn't look much older than Jim. Mr. Chan was a good guy; if you were sick he'd make a bowl of soup that tasted horrible and made you feel like a million bucks; if you were low on cash he'd let you run a tab until you were flush again.

"Listen," Jim was telling Chan. "If you don't have any money in Pittsburgh Industrial, now is the time to buy. Trust me on this, Chan, I don't want to see you take a bath."

"Yeah, right," Chan said. "The last time I listened to you, I lost my shirt in the market."

I sat down with them. "Hi, Jim. Hiya, Mr. Chan."

They both half stood and then sat back down. "Josephine," Chan said. "Would you take advice from this son of a bitch?"

I shrugged. I didn't know if he was conning Mr. Chan or giving him the genuine article. Selling fake stocks had taught Jim something about real stocks, and he had some money in the market himself. "I do," I said. "But I don't know if I should."

Chan laughed and went to get our dinner. Jim asked how I was coming along looking for the girl. I told him what I'd been doing so far, which was basically running into dead ends. One of Chan's sons, Albert, brought us a tureen of soup and two bowls. Like at Lenny's, we wouldn't order anything here. Jim had been going to Chan's for twenty years, and he'd get the best of everything.

When Albert was gone Jim ladled out the soup and said, "Well, if you want to find a drug addict, why don't you go where the drugs are?"

I looked at him. Drugs were everywhere.

He blew on his soup, cooling it down. "When you were using," he said, "where did you spend most of your time?"

"Huh," I said. I'd already been to Paul's. But that was nothing. There was a whole world of dope out there. It wasn't one neighborhood. It was like a string of islands, all over the city, where addicts and dealers got together. One island was on 103rd Street. The next one down was Seventy-seventh and Broadway, then Forty-second Street, then Fourteenth. Seventy-seventh Street was mostly Puerto Ricans, and 103rd Street was mostly old-timers. The West Side of Forty-second was a rougher crowd; I couldn't see Nadine there, but the East Side was a little more mixed, all types went there. . . .

I was surprised how easily it all came back to me. I'd tried hard to forget, but I still knew the other city, the dope-city, like the back of my hand.

"You know you're pretty clever, sometimes," I said to Jim. I tasted the soup and burned my tongue. I hadn't blown on it first.

"You're not so bad yourself," he said. We spent the rest of the dinner talking about a letter Jim had just gotten from Gary. He was coming to New York next month to work a stock angle with some big lawyers—he had met one of them on a ship to England and the first sucker had brought the rest of the marks in. Gary already had a few shills lined up, men who would play the part of satisfied investors, and he wanted Jim to be another one. So he had to go out and buy new suits, gray flannel. One of the other fellows had already rented an office, and Jim would help him furnish it to look like a brokerage house.

I half listened as we finished eating. Jim paid the check and we walked out, going toward Broadway.

When we were halfway down the block I thought of something. I stopped, turned around, and went back into Chan's. Chan was up at the cash register, yelling at another one of his sons in Chinese. I waited until he was done. Then I showed him the photo of Nadine and McFall and asked if he knew them.

He looked at the photo and scowled.

"Him, I know," Chan said. "Not her. He's not allowed in here, never again."

"Why not?" I asked.

"He brought a girl in here, looked like her, but not the same. The girl got sick in the bathroom. Drugs. Had to call an ambulance. And him, he just left her here. Just left her all alone to die. My wife, she stayed with her until the ambulance came. You know him?"

"Not exactly," I said. "I'm trying to find him."

"You ask me," Chan said, "stop looking. That's someone you don't want to find."

# Chapter Eleven

Bryant Park was probably a nice park, once. Two square blocks with benches and grass where housewives could walk their kids and their dogs and on weekends, their husbands. There had probably been thick grass on the ground and clean benches and big lovely trees to give shade and maybe some bright flowers in the spring. It was behind the big old public library, the famous one with the lions on Fifth Avenue and Forty-second Street. The library was probably nice, too, once. I guess it was still all right if you were a man. Jim went there a few times a week and he said it was one of his favorite places in the city.

But I'd been to the library once, and I'd seen as much male anatomy in one day as I had in my whole life before. I thought I'd take up reading as a new hobby after I got off dope and had time on my hands. After my trip to the library I figured I'd stick to stealing. The perverts had settled into the library just like the junkies had settled into Bryant Park. The park was where they came to enjoy the sunshine and make deals and catch up on gossip. And now no one bothered to keep up the grass or trim the trees or plant any flowers. The whole place smelled like piss and the benches were crumbling away and no square in their right mind would dream of walking through it.

I used to spend a lot of time in Bryant Park, but I hadn't been around for a few years. When I showed up all the junkies looked at me, trying to get a read on who I was and what I was up to. The sun was bright and every one of them squinted at me through it like they had never seen daylight before.

I walked around until I saw someone I knew. Monte. He was sitting on a bench in the shade of a big tree, smoking a cigarette. He wore a tan summer suit with a few spots on it and a wide-brimmed hat that looked like it had passed through a dozen men before it had come to him. It had been a good three years since I'd seen him in person, but he'd aged about thirty, and in all the wrong ways. He couldn't have weighed much more than a hundred pounds. His hair had thinned out, he had misplaced one of his front teeth, and there was a new scar just by his ear on the left side from a knife fight.

He was my husband.

I watched him for a while before he saw me, and a funny thing happened. I didn't see an old junkie in a worn-out suit anymore. Instead I saw a man ten years younger and forty pounds heavier, and the forty extra pounds were all muscle. His suit was spotless, like it always was, pressed just that morning, with a fresh white handkerchief in his breast pocket. Thick blond hair fell into his eyes no matter how much he combed it back because he couldn't sit still, he was always up and doing something, even if it was just straightening out a stack of papers or tapping his fingers on the table, working out his new plan.

And there was always a plan, a new one every few weeks. At first the plans were always how we would make some money and get out of Hell's Kitchen. Monte was going to get a job in a factory somewhere, or a job in sales; sales was a good deal because the harder you worked, the more money you could make. He knew a fellow who worked in a Cadillac dealership in New Jersey, and Monte was sure that if the fellow got him a job he could be taking home a hundred dollars a week.

Then the plans were about getting money for dope. One big score, because he couldn't hold down a regular job anymore. There was a house on Eighty-second and Park that was just ripe for the picking. Old couple, rich as sin, and they always left the window open at night.

The only problem was figuring out how to make it up to the third floor without anyone noticing. Or he was going to pull off a job with some boys from the neighborhood. These boys, they knew when the bagman made his pick-ups every week. It would be easy, all they had to do was get the bagman alone and the money was as good as theirs. A thousand dollars each, at least.

Soon the plans were all about kicking. The big plan was always for tomorrow, or next week. The plan was never for today. You mixed the dope with half water, shot it that way, and slowly increased the water until you were shooting plain water every day, and you'd never feel any pain at all. Or the plan was that Monte would go to Lexington, Kentucky, where there was a hospital that would give you a cure that'd make you never want to touch dope again. Next week, maybe. Or the week after.

And then the plan was just to get up in the morning. The plan was: today, I'll get out of bed. This afternoon, I'll take a bath. I'll comb my hair. By then the idea of putting on a clean suit was as far away as working at the Cadillac showroom had been.

We'd split up around five years before, during one of the other times I'd quit. It hadn't stuck that time—quitting dope—but I'd done the right thing and left the person who got me started on it. Not because I held it against him or wished him any ill will or because I didn't love him anymore, because none of that was true. Just because I had to. It was the only way.

"Monte."

"Joe!" He smiled when he saw me, and stood up and hugged me. I hugged him back, feeling his shoulder blades and the bumps of his spine through his suit.

"Jesus, Monte, you're a rail."

He laughed and we both sat down on the bench. "I know, I'm a little thin," he said. He looked at me. "You look good, Joe. You really do. I can tell you're clean."

"Yeah," I said. "About two years now."

Monte smiled. The teeth he had left were yellow and chipped, but it was still a good smile. He meant it. "I'm so happy, Joe. I mean, I never wanted—"

"I know," I said. "I know. It's my own fault, my own and no one else's. How is everything? Life treating you good?"

"Sure," he said. "It's okay. It's not too bad. How about you? What are you doing now?"

I shrugged. "A little of this and a little of that. I hit Tiffany's last week, did real good."

"That's great," Monte said. "So you're still up to your old tricks?"

"Yeah," I said. "Yeah."

"Good," he said, nodding. "Good."

"Hey. I saw Yonah the other day."

"Oh yeah?" Monte asked. "How's that old son of a bitch holding up?"

"Oh, he's okay," I answered. "He's the same. Same old Yonah."

"Hey, how's Shelley doing? I saw her photograph in the paper this morning. An ad for soap or something like that."

"She's good," I said. "She's good."

"She helping you out?" Monte asked. "Throwing a little money your way?"

"No," I said. "Why would she?"

Monte shook his head. "If it wasn't for you that kid would be dead. Dead a hundred times over. If it wasn't for you—"

"All right," I said. "All right. I know you don't like her. You never did."

Monte shrugged. "Nah, it ain't that. I just think you did enough for her, that's all. When's she gonna do something for you?"

I stiffened. "What do you think, she's making a million bucks modeling for the paper? She probably makes less than you. Besides, she doesn't owe me anything."

"Doesn't owe—"

I stopped him. "All right," I said again. "Enough."

We didn't say anything for a minute. Then Monte laughed. "It's like we're still married. Arguing about Shelley."

I laughed, too. "Yeah. It is."

We were quiet for another minute. Then I said, "Oh, I've got this new thing I'm working on. I'm looking for this girl. Her parents paid me to find her. I thought you might have seen her."

"That sounds good," Monte said. "You making some money?"

"Yeah. It's okay."

I showed him the picture of Nadine and McFall. He made a look on his face, a look like he'd just stepped in shit, that I was starting to recognize as McFall's calling card.

"Sure, I know Jerry. A real piece of work."

"Does he come around here?" I asked.

"Sometimes," Monte answered. "Not often."

"You know where he gets his stuff?" I asked.

Monte put his hand on my knee and we stopped talking for a second as a man in a neat gray suit walked by. You never knew who was the law. But you could tell he wasn't one of us.

After the man passed Monte shrugged. "It's funny— I don't know where he gets it. I mean, he's always got it, and as far as I know it's not from any of the regular guys, not the guys in Brooklyn or Harlem or anyone I know. But it's good."

"You've bought from him?" I asked. Monte sold junk himself, usually. It was how he got by.

"Sure, when I was dry myself."

"Well, how'd you get in touch with him? You got a phone number or something?"

"Nah." He shrugged. "I just ran into him, that's all."

"Can you tell me anything else about him, anything at all?"

Monte thought for a minute. When he did that he tilted his head to the right a little, just like he always had, and for a minute there I could have sworn it was fifteen years ago and we were kids, coming to Bryant Park for the first time. "Sometimes he hangs around with a guy you know," Monte said. "Skinny Harry. I think McFall's got him running errands for him, making deliveries, that kind of thing."

A big smile spread across my face.

"Jesus, Joe," Monte said. "You look like the cat that just ate the canary."

I felt like that cat, too. As far as I was concerned, the case was damn well over. The second thousand dollars was as good as mine.

"You know where I can find Harry?" I asked.

"Sure," Monte said. "He's at the Red Rooster down on Fourteenth just about every night. Hey, speaking of Harry, remember that time in Buffalo—" He started to laugh.

I laughed, too. "Oh, sure. That weasel really thought he'd gotten over on us. . . ."

That was all Monte had to say on the topic of Jerry McFall. And he had never seen Nadine before. We talked for a while more, trading old stories and adding in a few new ones. I pretended that he was the same old Monte and he, I guess, pretended that I was the same old Joe. We'd been together for close to ten years, which made it easy. Easy to pretend that Monte was young and strong and smart as a whip. That he still had all of his teeth and all of his brains and that his years on junk hadn't hurt him at all. That he was sick of Bryant Park and all the junkies, that he was going to kick tomorrow—maybe not tomorrow, tomorrow was no good, but next week for sure. That this new method he had was really going to do the trick, he was going to taper off and he would hardly be sick at all. That he was going to get a job in a factory in Brooklyn, his cousin worked there, he'd set Monte up for sure. That this time was going to be different, that this time it was going to work.

And it was easy to pretend that I was still listening. I nodded my head when he talked about kicking. Sure, I believed him, of course I did. Why wouldn't I? I had never heard this before, not me. It wasn't like I had said it all myself, a thousand times before. Because the thing is, when you meant it, you stopped talking about it. When I finally kicked I didn't say a word. I just did it. It was like when you talked about it you got the whole idea out of your system, and you could forget about it for a while. Talking about kicking was just another stop in the long conversation, along with science and finance.

It wasn't the drug itself that held him back, that made it all impossible. He could talk about withdrawal until the cows came home, but in the end, it wasn't so bad. A week of hell wasn't long. What made it impossible was the awful loneliness of going *out there,* alone. Here, with the other dope fiends, Monte had a place for himself. People knew who he was. *He* knew who he was. If Monte wasn't an addict, he'd be just another poor schmuck from Hell's Kitchen who never did a damn thing with his life. Just a guy who went to a dumb job every day and drank beer every night.

That's why you start, and that's why you stick with it, so you can finally be someone: a junkie.

When I left Monte I went around to all the newsstands in Times Square until I found the newspaper with the soap ad. It was a photo of Shelley, from the neck up, soap bubbles covering her shoulders. Here she was easier to recognize. She had a sly look on her face, like she was getting away with something, that I had seen a hundred times before. *It's not JUST a bubble bath,* a fancy script spelled out beneath her picture. *It's also a BEAUTY TREATMENT!*

At home I carefully cut out the picture and put it in Shelley's scrapbook next to the ad for the dress Yonah had given me. I only gave myself a few minutes to flip through the scrapbook before I went to find Harry.

# Chapter Twelve

alk about a joint. No band. No food. The Red Rooster was a long narrow room on Fourteenth Street with a bar and a few tables. A jukebox played some tinny-sounding swing. The place was half full and it was a rough enough crowd: one or two women who looked like streetwalkers, a dozen men in frayed suits and just as many in shirtsleeves, and a handful of young thugs in dungarees and undershirts.

Right off I spotted Skinny Harry, sitting alone at a table in the back. Skinny Harry wasn't really so skinny, now that he was reaching toward middle age. But he was still the same piece of trash he'd been since I first met him in 1939. His hair was thinning and slicked back from his head with grease, and he wore a shirt and slacks of no particular color and a red and black plaid hunting jacket. His beady little eyes were focused on a mug of beer. Harry's face turned blank when he spotted me, and he looked around for the nearest exit, but before he could make a run for it I reached his table and put my hand on his shoulder and pushed him back into his chair.

I sat down next to him, keeping a hand tight on his shoulder. "Harry," I said. The look on his face told me this would be easy.

"Listen, Joe, I know you think I tore you off that time in Buffalo—"

I cut him off. "Harry, I *know* you tore me off that time in Buffalo. I know you set me up, I know you owe me a wad of cash like you're never gonna see again. And you know it, too. I heard you spent it all paying a girl to beat you with a whip. That's disgusting, Harry. But that's not why I'm here."

He raised his eyebrows. "It's not?"

"No, I just need a favor. We're friends, aren't we, Harry?"

"Sure, sure we are, Joe." He looked ready to piss in his pants.

"And you can do me a favor, can't you? Wouldn't it be nice to get this Buffalo thing off your mind once and for all?"

"Of course, Joe, sure," he said quickly. "Anything, I'm good for it."

"Okay then. Jerry McFall. You know the guy?"

"Yeah, I know him."

"Good. Where is he?"

Harry hesitated. I could tell from his eyes he was making up a lie, and I didn't want to give him any time to work on it.

"Come on, Harry, you don't have to think about it. You want us to be square, or you want to spend the rest of your life looking over your shoulder?"

He wrinkled up his brow. "This would really square us, once and for all?"

"Absolutely, Harry," I lied. We'd never be square. "But you've got to tell me where he is, and it's got to be good."

"It's just that he asked me, really made me promise not to tell anyone—"

"But he didn't mean *me*, Harry, you know that. I don't count. You wouldn't be breaking your promise at all."

Harry slumped in his chair. I gave his shoulder a squeeze.

"Yeah, okay," he finally said. "The last I heard, he was staying at this place out in Sunset Park."

"Sunset Park? Where the hell is that?"

"Forty-fifth Street and Fifth Avenue, in Brooklyn. All the way out there. I don't remember the number but it's a brick building, apartments, right on the corner."

"You been there?"

He sighed. "Yeah, I been there. A few days ago. I went by just to say hi, to pal around, you know? And to bring him some clothes 'n' stuff."

"What's the story?" I asked. "Why's he laying so low?"

"What he told me was that someone thought he had ripped them off," Harry said with a smirk. "You know, in a dope deal. Of course, he said he hadn't done it, but he wanted to give everyone some time to cool off all the same."

"Who was it?" I asked. "Who'd he rip off?"

Harry shrugged. "He didn't say."

"But of course he didn't do it, right?"

Harry smiled. "I don't know, he said he didn't."

"How about a girl, Nadine? Is she with him?"

"Yeah, he's got a girl with him. A cute little blonde, young, real pretty." Harry's eyes glazed over at the thought of Jerry's cute little blonde. It was kind of disgusting.

I rolled my eyes. "All right," I said. "This better be good." I stood up to go.

"So this is it?" Harry said, looking up nervously. "I mean we're okay now, right?"

"Go to hell, Harry," I said. "We'll never be okay."

# Chapter Thirteen

Jim lived on Fifth Avenue, north of Washington Square Park, in a fancy apartment building that had just been built last year. The whole front of the lobby was all glass and it looked like a fishbowl. Jim wouldn't be there long. He moved two or three times a year, depending on what kind of work he was doing and what he could afford and what he felt like and who he wanted to be, or seem to be.

The doorman called upstairs by a house phone and told Jim with a straight face that a Miss Marlene Dietrich was here to see him. Jim said to send her on up. Naturally he took the time to put on a jacket and a hat before he answered the door.

He smiled when he saw who it was. He was in a good mood. That would help. "Hey Marlene. You wanna go get a drink or something?"

"No, thanks. But I was hoping you could do me a favor." I figured I better ease into this slowly. Jim had a thing about his car.

"Anything, Joe. Come on in." I followed Jim inside. His place was a good size and done up to the nines— sunken living room, new record player that played forty-fives, and all new furniture, streamlined like the sofa and the chairs were about to take flight. I sat down on a turquoise leather sofa while Jim fixed me a drink at the bar.

He joined me on the sofa with the drinks. The glasses had gold and turquoise seashells painted on them.

"Well," I began, "I finally got a good lead on Nadine Nelson."

"Great!" Jim smiled and clinked his glass against mine. He really seemed happy for me. "Where'd you track her down?"

I told him about Skinny Harry and our fun evening together. Jim knew Harry, and he laughed so hard he almost spit out his drink.

"So the thing is," I said, "Harry tells me they're in Brooklyn. Like way far out in Brooklyn. I'm not sure if the subway even goes out there."

Jim stopped laughing.

"And I really need to get there as soon as possible."

Jim stopped smiling.

"So I was hoping I could borrow your car for a while."

He looked down at the floor and thought for a minute. "I could call you a cab," he suggested. "I'll even pay for it. A taxi'll go out there, no problem."

"Right," I said. "Thanks. That's really nice of you. But the thing is, a taxi would really stick out around there. I mean, I might have to watch the place for a while, wait until they come out. I don't want to scare them off. I need to let the parents know where the girl is while she's still there. If they split, I'm right back where I started. So I definitely don't want them seeing a taxi out front waiting for them."

"That's true," Jim said. "That's true. But you know, the Rocket 88 would stand out, too. I mean, a new car. In a neighborhood like that."

"Right," I said. "But not really. Not so much."

"You have a good record, right?" He was dead serious. He really loved that car.

"Perfect. Never even a ticket," I lied.

"You're sure?"

I took my license out of my purse and showed it to him. "Call Motor Vehicles," I said. It was too late to call Motor Vehicles. If it wasn't, I wouldn't have said it.

Jim laughed. But he did glance at the phone. "Okay," he finally said. "But you gotta go nice and slow—"

"I won't speed," I promised.

"And you gotta be careful when you park."

"I won't park within ten feet of another car," I said.

"And no drinks," he said sternly. "No drinks, no food, cigarettes, nothing like that."

"Jim," I said, "I will treat your car like it was my newborn babe."

"Okay, okay." Jim let out a long breath and tried not to frown. "Warm it up first. And watch where you park. Try not to park it outside. And don't forget to lock it up if you leave it. But don't leave it, Joe. Don't leave the car alone. Not unless you have to. And call me when you get back to the city. Just to let me know you're all right."

"You mean that the car's all right," I said.

"No," Jim said. "That you're all right."

Jim insisted on taking me out to eat before I drove to Brooklyn. But I wanted to get going soon, and so even though Jim wanted to go to Le Bouche, which of course is the best place to eat late at night if you like French food like snails and liver, he settled for a hash house in Sheridan Square that was open all night. It wasn't up to his usual standards. The coffee was awful and the waitress didn't know Jim's first name. Across the room a man was telling a story in a loud voice about the funny time he had with Rita Hayworth in Cannes.

"For Christ's sake," Jim said, scowling at his omelet. "Who the hell is this guy trying to impress?"

"I don't know," I said with my mouth full. "Just forget it."

"I mean, who does he think he is?" Jim fumed. "*Where* does he think he is, for cryin' out loud—the Stork Club?"

"I. Don't. Know." I said.

Jim craned his neck to give the man a dirty look. "Hey," he said when he turned around. "Isn't that Shelley?"

I looked over. The man who was telling the story was sitting at a table across the room. He was a middle-aged man in a black three-piece suit, overweight and half bald, with a big diamond pin on his tie and an even bigger diamond on his little finger. Sitting with him was Shelley.

At least I thought so. Then I looked again and I wasn't sure. She hardly looked like Shelley at all. She looked more like the girl wearing the black dress in the ad Yonah had given me. Her hair was cut short and bleached platinum, and she was wearing a modest black dress with a tiny black hat over her white hair. She had on shiny red lipstick and a little bit of black makeup around her eyes. She laughed at the man's story like it was the funniest thing she had ever heard and leaned toward him, keeping her back straight and her chest out.

It was Shelley. But it was like she'd been to some kind of a spa where they took every little bit of Hell's Kitchen right out of her. It was her, but it wasn't.

I was wondering whether I should say hi or not when she finally saw me. Her eyebrows went up in surprise— I guess I was the last person she expected to see—and then she smiled a little, and nodded toward the ladies' room. I waited until she stood up and then I did, and we met in the bathroom.

We hugged each other. I hadn't seen her in close to a year. Shelley was my sister. She was five years younger, and for a long time there it looked like Shelley might turn out like me. She was hanging around with the same people and getting into the same trouble and sniffing the same dope. But somehow, while I was busy wondering where my next fix was coming from, she pulled herself out of it. She stopped hanging out with the old crowd. Moved out of Hell's Kitchen, where we grew up, and got a job checking coats at a supper club where she'd meet the right people. Now my scrapbook was almost full of pictures of her from magazines and playbills from shows she'd been in. She even had photos printed up, glossy pictures of her face with a thick coat of makeup and her name underneath, her stage name—Shelley Dumere. I guess Flannigan had a low-class ring to it, and besides, it wouldn't do any good for anyone to know who she was related to or who she used to be.

"Jesus, Joe," she said, with a big smile like the one in her photo. A big fake smile. "It's good to see you. But I've only got a minute." She started fixing her makeup in the mirror. I leaned against the wall and watched her. She didn't just powder her face like most women did. Instead she put a spot here and a spot there, carefully, like she was painting a picture.

"Who's the guy?" I asked. I couldn't help but smile. I was happy to see her.

"He's producing a show," she said. She sounded excited. "Not theater. That ain't nothing now. A television show!"

"That's great," I said. "What kind of a role is it?"

"It's this new show. It's gonna be on every Thursday night at eight o'clock, it's part of the Vita-Crunch Cereal Family Hour. They don't have a name decided on yet, but it's all about this goofy broad, a housewife, and all the funny things she does. You know, like burn dinner for her husband and things like that. I think I'm perfect for it!" She looked in the mirror and smiled at herself. "You know, there's a lot of out-of-work actors in this town, Joe. I know people who'd kill for any kind of work. It ain't easy to get a part like this."

"I bet," I said. "You still taking acting classes?"

"Nah," she said, dabbing powder on her forehead just so. "Honestly, Joe, now that I'm in show business, I see how it really works. It's all about who you know.

I mean I can act just as good as any of those other whores, right?"

"Sure," I said. "Sure you can."

She frowned at herself in the mirror and began touching up around her eyes with a black eye pencil. "How about you?" she asked. "What are you and Jim doing out so late?"

"Actually," I said, "I've been looking for someone—you might know them. This girl, her parents hired me to find her—"

She raised her eyebrows. "What are you, like a private dick now?" She laughed. "Can you imagine? I mean you, of all people! Well, anyway, who is it?"

I showed her the picture of Nadine Nelson and Jerry McFall.

She glanced at the picture. "You know, I think I might have met him before. Years ago."

"Oh yeah? Where?"

"I don't know, Joe. It could have been anywhere. He just looks familiar, that's all. I mean, you know I don't hang around with people like that no more. I mean, *anymore*. Jeez, Joe, if you're gonna be a private dick you gotta learn who to ask what." She laughed again.

"Yeah," I said. "Anyway, everything's good? I saw you in the paper a few times—"

She smiled. "Oh yeah? Did you see the one for soap?

I looked pretty good, right?" She put away the eye pencil and took out a lipstick in a gold tube. "Anyway, everything's been real good, Joe. *Real* good. This guy, he thinks I'm gonna be a television star." She dabbed at her lips with the lipstick. "Whadaya think of that? Me, a television star!" She looked pretty pleased with the idea. She put the lipstick back in her pocketbook and stood up to face me. "Well, I guess I ought to get back. He's probably wondering where I've been."

"Okay," I said. She didn't have to say that I shouldn't let on that I knew her in front of the producer. That went without saying. We hugged again.

"I'm sorry it's been so long," she said. "But I'll call you real soon, Joe, okay? I promise. You still at the same place?"

"Yeah," I said. "The Sweedmore."

She smiled. "Okay. I'll call you soon."

"Sure," I said. "Anytime."

I knew she wouldn't call, and I didn't blame her, either. Putting a few dinners on the table and buying a few dresses didn't make up for a long list of disappointments. Because that's what junkies do; they disappoint. They say they'll show up for dinner at eight and they come at eight the next morning. They say they'll take care of the rent and then they shoot the money up their arm. They say they'll always be there for you and then they nod out on a park bench when you need them the most. We didn't have a father around, and our mother wasn't good for much. It was just the two of us. There wasn't a lot of room for those kinds of disappointments. I was clean now, but there was no reason for her to forgive me. I wouldn't have.

Shelley walked out of the ladies' room and I waited another minute before I left, so it wouldn't look like we were walking out together. By the time I got back to my table she'd already sat back down with the producer. Across the room I could hear him telling a new story, this one about his latest airplane trip to Los Angeles.

"Should I go over and say hello?" Jim asked. "I haven't seen her in ages."

"Nah," I said. "She can't afford to be seen with the likes of us."

Jim looked at me for a minute. "Hey," he said. I guess he was going to say more, something bright and cheerful, but there really wasn't anything to say.

As we finished our omelets I snuck a few glances at Shelley's table. Another man had dropped by their table, a man about my age, and I wondered if he was another of her boyfriends. Most girls would have lost both guys if they were in the same place at the same time, but Shelley had always been good at that. She never slipped up, always played it off perfectly. I watched as she gave exactly equal attention to each man, first looking at the one and then the other like she was watching a tennis match.

Jim paid the bill and we left. We went to the garage and got the car, and then Jim walked home and I started driving toward Brooklyn.

# Chapter Fourteen

The black Rocket 88 was polished spotless inside and out, but while I was going over the Brooklyn Bridge I noticed something sticking out from under the passenger-side seat. A piece of brown paper. At a red light on Atlantic Avenue I leaned down and pulled it out. What I'd seen was the edge of a brown paper package, tied with string.

*Hope it fits* was written on the front in black pen.

I opened it up. It was the dress Jim told me about, the one he bought from Mick. I looked at it. It was from Bergdorf's all right, the real thing. Midnight blue with a tight waist and a full skirt. It would fit just fine.

The car behind me honked. The light had changed, and I got moving. I felt pretty high on myself driving around in a new car like that. I thought maybe if this all panned out and I did get the other thousand I'd buy myself a car. I'd never had one before, not all my own. Of course I wouldn't get a new car like this, that'd be all the money I made. Something a little older. But still nice. Jim could help me pick it out.

The drive took a little under an hour. I thought I knew the way, but halfway through Brooklyn I had to stop at a gas station and buy a map. I was going to fill up the car, too, but when I saw they were asking twenty-five cents a gallon I figured I'd just give Jim a few pints of blood instead. Finally I found Forty-fifth Street and Fifth Avenue, the Brooklyn versions. Sunset Park in Brooklyn was pretty much like any residential neighborhood in Manhattan, but with more trees. Lots of limestone houses that could be nice if anyone cared and lots of low apartment buildings that never would be. Just like Harry promised, there was a brick apartment building on the corner of Forty-fifth and Fifth. It wasn't a big place, four stories with probably two apartments on each floor. There were fire escapes on both sides. The entrance was on Forty-fifth. I drove by. A plain glass door and a bank of mailboxes built into the wall. Not much to come home to.

I parked across the street on Forty-fifth, a few yards down from the building, where I had a nice clear view in the rearview mirror. All the curtains were closed. After watching the windows for a few minutes I walked over and checked the mailboxes. Kanstowski, Koen, Dubinski, and a bunch of blanks.

I settled in to watch the building. McFall and Nadine were in there somewhere, and eventually they'd have to come out. Once I was sure they were there I'd call her parents and see what they wanted to do—if they wanted to come see her themselves or call the police or have me try to talk to her. I kept my eyes on the door. No one came in or out of the building. In fact no one seemed to be awake on the whole block, and after a while it was hard to stay awake. I turned on the radio. On one station there was a news report about the communists. They were everywhere, and if we didn't look out they'd get our kids. Sure. Like the drug pushers with mustaches. On another station was a detective story. I listened for a while. The good guy won. The bad guy lost. The girl didn't do much of anything at all. After a few hours I started to doze off, but every few seconds I opened my eyes to make sure nothing was going on.

At five-thirty the sun began to come up. Soon enough people started leaving their houses to go to work, which made it easy to stay awake. By eight the working people thinned out and the block was quiet again. I dozed.

At ten after eleven I woke up and checked the rearview mirror.

I had struck gold.

A pretty girl walked out of the brick building on the corner, wearing dungarees and a man's shirt tied at the waist. She was a small blonde, young, and wore her hair in a ponytail.

It wasn't Nadine. But right next to her was Jerry McFall.

It was funny to see the guy in person again. He looked just like I remembered, except he was nothing at all like I had in mind. Physically, he was the same. Tall and thin with a narrow face. He wore gray trousers and a yellow shirt, no jacket, and a gray fedora on his head. A little flashy, maybe, but not over the top.

What I didn't expect was for the guy to look happy. He had a smile on his face and put his hand gently on the small of the girl's back as they walked. There was no swagger. No sneer. If I hadn't known better I would have figured him for a regular working guy, a guy who loved his girl and was happy with the world. Maybe worked at a trade: a carpenter, a stonemason. Good at his job. Got on with his neighbors. Everyone liked him. I could see why women fell for him again and again. They like that in a guy. I knew I did.

But I knew—this was a guy who wasn't good at anything. A guy who would lie to a woman, bully her, and if that didn't work, beat her to get her into bed. A guy who was going to take that nice-looking girl walking around with him and turn her into a street whore.

I thought of the first time I had met him. For a minute, I wanted to kill the guy. Or myself. But then it passed.

Once they were around the corner I got out of the car and followed. I was sure McFall wouldn't remember me. As long as I wasn't too obvious I didn't need to worry about them seeing me.

I walked around the corner and I spotted them down the block. McFall slipped his hand off her back and down her arm, then down to hold her hand. The girl smiled. They crossed Fifth Avenue and walked down to a little coffee shop on the corner of Fifth and Forty-sixth. I waited across the street. Half an hour later they walked out holding hands. They stopped at a grocery store, left with one bag each, and then went back to the brick building.

Just before they went inside, I stopped him.

"Jerry McFall," I said.

They both stopped and turned around. For the first time, I saw something on McFall's face like the look that was in his photo. This was the Jerry McFall I remembered, the one Monte and Yonah and the girls in the Royale had told me about.

He didn't say anything. The girl looked from Jerry to me and back again, confused.

"Jerry McFall," I said again. "Can I talk to you for a minute?"

He stared at me. The sun hit his eyes and he was squinting. I didn't move. He turned and whispered something to the girl and handed her the groceries. She turned and went inside.

"I'm looking for Nadine Nelson," I said. "Her parents paid me to find her. The last anyone heard she was with you."

He still didn't talk. It's a good trick—intimidates the hell out of the other guy. It almost worked on me. But not quite.

"I don't know what else you're up to," I said. "And I don't care. All I want is Nadine."

Finally he spoke. His voice was like I remembered it: kind of syrupy and smooth but also angry. "I ain't Jerry McFall," he said. "And I don't know any *Nadine*."

He said her name like it was a curse. He turned to walk back into the building.

"Hey." I grabbed his arm and tried to turn him around. "All I want to know is—"

He turned around all right. Turned around and slugged me right in the gut. I fell down to the ground, gagging.

I'd be okay. But I wasn't okay then. I lay on the sidewalk, curled up around my stomach.

He kicked me lightly on the back.

"I told you," he said. *"I ain't Jerry McFall."*

He turned and went back in the building. I lounged around on the sidewalk for a minute until I could breathe okay and I was sure I wasn't going to be sick. An old lady in black walked by on her way back from the market, with a shopping cart full of a thousand bags of groceries. She looked down at me.

"Goddamned drunks," she said, and kept walking.

By the time I got home it was two o'clock in the afternoon. I was sick and tired and worn out. I called Jim from Lavinia's phone, told him I was all right, and told him the car was all right. Then I took off my clothes and went right to bed.

I slept like the dead.

# Chapter Fifteen

The next morning I woke up to a heavy knock on the door. I sat up, and felt an awful pain at my waist. I lifted up my pajamas and looked at my belly. A purple bruise had grown where I took one from McFall the day before. It was a solid punch but I'd taken worse. The purple color would last awhile but the pain wouldn't last longer than the end of the day.

In the time it took me to get to the door the knock grew to a steady thud that was close to bringing the whole building down. I knew who it was. The cops. No one else would be beating down my door at nine in the morning. No one else ever had.

I answered the door in my pajamas. Two cops, one in a uniform, one in a cheap suit and a porkpie hat, pushed their way in as soon as I had the door unlocked.

"Hey Springer," I said to the cheap suit. "What's the good word?"

"It ain't your name, Flannigan," he said. The two men looked around my apartment, hoping to find maybe a corpse on the bed and a bag of dope on the coffee table. I'd known Springer as long as I could remember. He used to be a beat cop at the Fifty-fourth Street station, where I'd grown up. Now he was a homicide detective, but he still liked to keep in touch with his old pals from the neighborhood—like when his rent was due, for example. He was a big guy with a meaty face that only laughed if there was someone to laugh at. He didn't like me and I didn't like him and that was fine. The uniform I had never seen before. He was younger than me, and looked like an ex-boxer, or just a guy crazy for fighting. Not too tall, plenty wide, and a battered face that probably hadn't been much to begin with.

I walked over to the hot plate and put on the percolator. The cops started poking around the room, looking around at the empty glasses and magazines on the coffee table.

"So what's the dope on Jerry McFall," Springer said. "What'd he do, take a nickel off you? Stand you up for a date?"

The thug snickered. Springer smiled. He was pretty proud of his wit.

"I don't know any McFall," I said.

"That's funny," Springer said. "A hell of a lot of people say you've been looking around for him lately."

"So what?" I said. "Since when is looking for someone against the law?"

"Don't crack wise with me, Josephine," Springer said, angry now. "Shut your mouth or I'll shut it for you."

I didn't crack wise with him again. Instead I went to my purse and found the envelope I always kept with me. Inside was a crisp twenty-dollar bill.

"All right," I said to Springer. "I get it. The Policemen's Ball is coming up." I took the twenty out of the envelope and handed it to him. He took it and stuck it in his pocket. But he didn't go anywhere.

"Come on, Springer," I pleaded. "Look at this place—that's the best I can do." I had the real money, the $925.50 left over from the Nelsons, under a floorboard that was sealed shut under the bed. The floorboard looked good and they'd never find it.

"Thanks for the donation, Joe," he said, looking sour. "But it ain't gonna help you this time."

That was when I knew something was wrong. I sat down and drank a cup of coffee while they looked through my room. They covered all the spots a dumb thief would have hidden something: under the sofa, top shelf of the closet, inside the sugar jar. They had lots of fun in my underwear drawer, too. Then they got a little rougher and knocked the cups out of the cabinet and emptied the drawers onto the floor. They didn't find anything because there was nothing to find.

"If you're looking for dope," I said finally, "you can forget it. I'm clean and you know it."

"We ain't looking for dope," Springer said. "I don't give a shit about that. We're looking for a gun."

I was slow that morning. "Why would you be looking for a gun?"

"Because someone killed Jerry McFall last night," Springer said.

I looked at him.

"Yeah, that's right," he went on. "I bet you're real shocked, Joe. I bet you're just heartbroken. I got it, and you can wipe that damn look off your face now."

I tried to wipe off whatever look I had on my face.

"Jerry McFall was shot last night," he said. "And seeing as you've spent so much time looking around for him lately, we're thinking you're good for the shooting. A nice old lady even saw you hanging around the building earlier in the day. I got a tip to check you out, Flannigan, and I started asking around."

I didn't know what to say. So for a good long time I didn't say anything at all.

"Put some clothes on," Springer finally said, sick of waiting for my witty comeback. "You're coming with us."

# Chapter Sixteen

In the car on the way to the precinct I told Springer about the Nelsons. I explained that the only reason I was looking for McFall was because the Nelsons had hired me to find their daughter, and she used to go with him. I gave him their phone numbers and the address of Mr. Nelson's office.

"Sure," Springer said, and let out a laugh. The uniform chuckled, too. I wasn't sure if he even knew what he was chuckling at, or just did whatever his boss did. "You expect me to believe that out of everyone in New York City, they hired a junkie whore like you to find their daughter? Don't treat me like a jerk, Josephine, that's all I ask of you. Don't treat me like a fool."

While we drove Springer told me that McFall had been found dead in a girl's apartment in Sunset Park last night at about eight o'clock. The girl, who he'd picked up in a bar a few days before, had invited McFall to stay with her. She'd gone out to have dinner with a girlfriend and when she came back he was dead, shot through the chest. Springer got a tip that I was involved and he started asking around. He wouldn't say where the tip came from.

I started to feel sick.

Springer took me up to the old station on Fifty-fourth. "Hello Detective, Josephine," the desk sergeant said, nodding to both of us when we came in. "Hey Phillips," I said, forcing a smile. In fact I recognized a few fellows there, cops and the men and women they'd arrested, but it wasn't really a good time for catching up. Springer yanked me through to an interrogation room with a steel table and four steel chairs and no windows. I'd been in plenty of rooms like it before, maybe even the exact same room.

"You've been in this room before, Joe," Springer said, lighting a cigarette. He sat across from me in one of the steel chairs. "Two or three years back. Remember that? You sat right there and you wouldn't say a god-damned word. Not even when cold turkey started coming on and you started sweating and shaking and you threw up all over your dress. Remember?"

"Sure," I said. "I remember."

"What'd you get," Springer said, exhaling smoke from his cigarette. I would have liked one myself but I wasn't going to ask. "Thirty days? Ninety?"

"Thirty. Obstructing justice."

He nodded and looked down at the ashtray. "How about the time before that? We had you for boosting, what was it?"

"Dresses," I answered. "From Saks Fifth Avenue."

He smiled. "Right, sure. And what'd you get for that?"

"Six months," I told him. I stayed as cool as I could. I'd had fun with Springer before. But I didn't want him to think I was having fun with him now. This was a whole new ball game, one with different rules.

"You want a cigarette?" he asked, like he suddenly realized he wasn't being a gentleman.

"Yeah. Thanks." He shook one out of the pack, put it in his mouth, lit it, and handed it to me. I tried to hold my hand steady as I took it. He moved the ashtray to the middle of the table. "And before that?" he asked.

"Possession of a controlled substance," I answered. "Six months. Before that, aiding and abetting. You remember, the Minelli thing?"

Springer laughed. "Sure, I remember. You almost went away for a good long time for that one."

I laughed a little, too, even though I didn't feel like laughing. "I was lucky. The judge was pretty hip."

"What else? I don't want to go and get your file, Joe. It's on my desk under a heap of papers and I won't be happy if I've got to go find it."

I thought for a minute. "Possession, I think two more

135

times. Soliciting—I don't even know how many times. Four, maybe five. Theft, back when I was about eighteen."

Springer nodded and looked at me with a strange look on his face, a look that was almost kind. "You were just a kid then. You know, Joe, you're pretty good at what you do. Only two theft charges in a whole lifetime of stealing. That's a hell of a lot better than most of the characters we see around here."

"Thanks," I said.

He looked at me again for a long moment. It was almost like he was thinking. "You know I always thought you were smart, Joe," he finally said. "Always thought it was a shame, how things turned out for you. You never really got a chance in life, did you, with your mother and all? You were just a kid when you started turning tricks, trying to put food on the table, trying to look after Shelley. I'm talking about before you got messed up on dope, before you even met Monte. You could have run off a thousand times but you didn't want to leave your sister behind. I know that. You did all right by her—got her those acting classes, got her out of Hell's Kitchen, set her up with that job at the El Sahara. Why, I saw her in the paper just a few days ago, made me kind of proud. But you—you never got a break, did you? You married that bum and got yourself hooked on dope and—"

"Thanks," I said. "But it hasn't been so bad."

"Anyway," he said, still looking at me. "What I'm

trying to tell you is that what you've gotten yourself into now—well, it's not anything like those other times. You've gotten off easy so far. Never done more than six months or so. But this McFall thing—this is murder. This is a whole different can of worms, Joe. If you go to court for this, you're going away for a long time, maybe even getting the chair, no matter the judge likes your looks or how much you cry up on the stand. You're older now. None of those tricks are gonna work anymore."

"I know," I told him, stubbing out the cigarette. None of those tricks had worked for a long time. "But I didn't kill McFall. I'm telling you the God's honest truth, Springer, I didn't do it."

He smiled and lit me another cigarette. "Joe. You're not listening to me. What I'm telling you is that if you tell me the truth now, the whole truth, I can cut a deal for you with the DA. I'll do everything I can to keep you out of the chair, you have my word on that. Maybe we can even get you a nice short sentence, get some mitigating circumstances in there. I'm sure they were there. I'm sure you had a reason. I know you, Joe. You wouldn't have done this without a reason, a good one. And there's your background—your mother, how you sent Shelley to acting classes, all that sort of thing, they'll take that into account."

I told him about the Nelsons again, and everything I had done since then, and all I had found out about Nadine Nelson and Jerry McFall. It was no secret to him that Monte and Yonah were using and that prostitution was going on at Rose's and the Royale, so there was no reason to hold anything back. I told him everything.

He laughed again. "Josephine," he said. "Come on." Then he stood and picked up the ashtray and threw it at the wall behind me. "GODDAMN IT, Joe!" he screamed. "You tell me the truth this very minute or I swear to God, I SWEAR TO GOD I'll knock your fucking head off."

I sat perfectly still and looked at the table and didn't say a word. The ashes from the ashtray settled down all over the room like snow. Springer sat back down. His face was bright red. He took a deep breath. "Get the ashtray for me, will you, Joe."

I picked up the ashtray and put it back down where it had been in the middle of the table.

"Another cigarette?" he said, lighting one for himself.

"Sure," I said. "Thanks."

He lit one for me and his face faded back to its regular pink. Just as he was handing me the cigarette there was a knock on the door. Springer said to come in and a young cop opened the door and poked his head in and nodded out toward the hall.

"Excuse me." Springer went into the hall for a second with the kid. He came back in and sat down.

"O'Reilly called those phone numbers you gave us, Joe. There's nothing there."

"What?" I asked. "What do you mean, nothing there?"

He shrugged. "They're bogus, Joe. Whatever pals you were hoping would cover for you, their numbers were disconnected. Guess they spent the bill money on dope. There are no Nelsons, and we both know it."

For a minute I didn't say anything. It took a minute to sink in.

*There are no Nelsons.*

"It's impossible," I finally said. "Springer, they're real. I swear to God, I'll find them. I'll bring them down here—"

There are no Nelsons. Which meant I was left holding the whole bag. For the first time I saw myself through Springer's eyes. I didn't look good.

Their phone must have gone out of order. Phones go out of order all the time. Or maybe the stupid kid Springer had sent to make the call didn't know how to dial a phone number.

"It's like I told you," Springer said, looking right at me. "The sooner you tell me the truth, the better. No one's buying this story about someone paying you to find a girl."

"But I'll find them," I said, trying to sound more sure than I felt. "I'll find them and—"

Springer held up his hands to shut me up. "Come on, Joe. It's bullshit, you know it and I know it. It's like I said—what kind of people would hire *you* to find their daughter? Come on. Now, I don't have any evidence against you. Not yet. There's nothing tying you to the death, and that's a fact. So I've got to let you go now."

I stood up but he waved me back down with his hand. I sat back down.

"On the other hand," he continued, "it isn't looking so good. I know you've been looking for the fellow, and I've got witnesses for that. You could say you've got nothing to do with the man, and that's fine. But someone else might look at the fact that you know some of the same people, he's a dealer, you're a junkie, and see a deal gone wrong. That's the way I see it, and that's the way a jury'll see it, too. You know it and I know it. This is it for you, Joe. You're not getting out of this one."

Finally he told me to go, with a lot of threats about keeping my nose clean and how they'd be keeping their eyes on me and not to do anything stupid and so on.

I went outside and walked to the nearest pay phone.

I called the Nelsons at home. An operator picked up the line.

"I'm sorry," she said. "That number's been disconnected."

"Are you sure?" I asked. "Because I don't think so. I just don't think that could have happened."

"Ma'am," she said, getting annoyed, "I'm sure."

I hung up and called Mr. Nelson's office. An operator got on the line again. I hung up.

I took a taxi back to First Avenue, where Jim's car was parked, and then I drove down to 28 Fulton. The whole way I thought about what Springer had said: *You expect me to believe that out of everyone in New York City, they hired a junkie whore like you to find their daughter?*

When you put it like that, I had some trouble swallowing it myself.

# Chapter Seventeen

At the building on Fulton Street, the same doorman opened the door and the same fellow sat behind the counter and the same elevator operator brought me up to the fifth floor.

The door to Mr. Nelson's office was unlocked. I went inside and looked around.

My hands started to shake, and I felt sick to my stomach.

The desk was gone. So was the leather sofa and the typewriter and the rug and the telephone and the paintings on the walls. So was the pretty girl. All that was left was a phone cord sticking out of the wall in a dingy room.

I went through to the second room. It was empty. The sun was shining in through the window and I could see dust floating in the air. I turned around, and my footsteps echoed in the empty space.

I began to feel dizzy, and I sat down on the cold wood floor for a minute until the room stopped spinning.

It was like no one had ever been there at all.

My hands were still shaking as I took the elevator back down. I asked the fellow behind the counter what had happened to Mr. Nelson.

He frowned. "Mr. Nelson?"

"The lawyer," I said. I was surprised at the sound of my own voice. It sounded like I was begging for something. "The lawyer on the fifth floor."

The man looked at me from below his smart blue cap. "Nelson . . . let me check the book." He took a black loose-leaf binder out from a drawer and thumbed through it. "Nation?" he suggested.

"No."

"Norman?" he tried.

"Nelson," I said again. "I'm sure. It's Nelson."

He looked some more and then shook his head again. "Sorry, Miss. No Nelson here."

"Fifth floor," I said. "Last office."

He looked confused. "That office has been empty for months now. Sorry, lady. I don't know what to say."

What had happened was this: Jerry McFall had stolen a fair amount of dope from someone and they wanted it back. They wanted it back over Jerry's dead body. But they didn't know where he was. If they'd looked themselves, they would have left themselves wide open to the cops, just like I had. So they got two people—out-of-work actors, retired con men, friends who owed them a favor, it didn't really matter—two people to pose as the Nelsons. They thought Jerry and Nadine were still together, so they had me look for the girl. It was an easier pill to swallow—no one would have an honest reason for wanting to find Jerry McFall. So they asked me to look for the girl, and gave me a thousand dollars. The dope Jerry stole must have been worth at least five times that, so it was worth it. Now they'd gotten their dope back, gotten rid of McFall, and left me holding the bag.

When I left 28 Fulton I drove around for a while, because I liked to drive, and because my hands were still shaking and after talking to the doorman my teeth were chattering, too, and there wasn't much else I could do in that state. I drove without really paying attention to where I was, and after I had calmed down a little I was surprised to find that I was on Forty-second Street. Right next to Bryant Park.

I parked by a fire hydrant, but I didn't get out of the car.

I had a craving like I hadn't felt in years. Every muscle in my body felt weak, and I felt something sour come up in my throat. Like my last taste of dope had been eight hours ago instead of two years. Like I'd never kicked at all.

Monte was in the park. I was sure of it. He'd give me a taste. He'd give it to me and he'd be glad to do it. I could stay with him until Springer came to get me or I took my last shot, whichever came first. Jim would shed a few tears, so would Monte and a few others, but not too many, and not for long. Shelley—well, she'd be better off without me. She'd made that clear enough. I'd done what I could for her and now I was just a problem for her, an embarrassment. No one would miss me.

The odds were against me in every way. If I could win with this McFall business, chances were I'd slip up and get on dope again. Almost everyone did. I was no better than Yonah or Monte or Cora, and they'd probably kicked a hundred times between them. And if I got hooked again, I wouldn't have much longer to live. I was sure about that. Some people were lucky—they never bought stuff that was too pure or cut with poison, never got caught ripping someone off, never got busted by the cops. But I'd never had any luck that wasn't bad.

Sometimes when I was a kid, charity ladies would

come around to Hell's Kitchen, rich ladies from uptown, and they'd pick out the kids who had special talents or who were extra cute and they'd try to help them: buy the kids clothes and food, help them in school, make sure things weren't too bad at home. Sometimes these ladies even adopted kids from Hell's Kitchen. But they sure never lifted a finger for me. I figured they knew what everyone else knew: there was no hope for Josephine Flannigan. I'd heard people say that when they were little they wanted to be a nurse or a schoolteacher or something like that. But I always knew I'd never be a nurse or a schoolteacher. No one ever thought I had a chance in hell of making it to twenty, let alone thirty, and right now someone, somewhere, was betting that I wouldn't make it to forty.

But the thing was, I wanted to decide for myself. I didn't want Springer or Monte or drugs or anything or anyone else to decide for me. I didn't have much to live for, that was true. But what I had was mine. I'd earned it the hardest way I knew how. And I was going to keep it until I was ready to give it up.

I was going to find out who had set me up and killed McFall. And when I did, I wasn't going to take him to Springer, either. I was going to take care of him myself.

I found a legal parking spot nearby and walked past the park to the library. My hands were still shaking and my knees were weak but I could ignore that. Inside the library I tried not to look at any single men too closely, and I found the reference desk and asked the librarian if she had a directory of lawyers who practiced in New York City. She glared at me. I had interrupted a good reading of *Murder in Manhattan*, the paperback novel on the desk in front of her.

"Have you tried the phone book?" she asked. "Or do you mean something like *Who's Who*? Or the *Social Register*?"

"I mean all three," I said, trying to sound as high and mighty as she had. I hadn't thought of the phone book.

She smirked. "I'll get you all three." She rummaged around behind her desk for a while and then put three heavy books on the table. I opened the first one and she shook her head.

"Over there," she said. She pointed to a desk across the room and I lugged the books over.

Nathaniel Nelson wasn't in the *Social Register*, or *Who's Who*. But he was right there in the Manhattan phone book. *Nathaniel Nelson, Nelson & Associates. 667 Madison Avenue.*

# Chapter Eighteen

67 Madison was a modern glass building that stretched up farther than I could see without craning my neck. I figured I'd have to go through a few office girls to get to Mr. Nelson. I didn't figure four. The first receptionist was right there when you walked into the building. She was easy; told me to take the elevator up three flights, take a right, and ring the buzzer. I did, and I was let into a big room with fancy sofas and a thick carpet by a brunette in pink. She was a little more inquisitive. What was my business with Mr. Nelson? Personal. What was my name? Miss Josephine Flannigan. I looked for a reaction. There was none. She made a call, and then instructed me to take the elevator up two more flights. There I would make a left and look for the door marked "Executive." On the other side I was met by a

blonde in baby blue. The girls got prettier as I climbed up the ladder.

My business? Personal. My name? Flannigan. Didn't ring a bell with her, either, unless the office girls were also actresses now. I was glad I wasn't one of them. Glad I wasn't going to work for a big shot every day, opening his mail and picking up his shirts and generally making his life livable, waiting for him to notice me. He never would.

The blonde conferred by phone with someone else for a minute and then escorted me through another door. The girl behind the desk in this room should have been in Hollywood. She had thick black hair and eyes you could drown in. She wore a black suit that looked sewn on. The room was paneled in mahogany and all the furniture was brown leather. I figured this was the end of the line, unless next was a girl in a swimsuit in a room covered in floor-to-ceiling mink.

"Miss Flannigan," the brunette said with a smile and a voice like a violin. "How can I help you?"

"I'd like to see Mr. Nelson."

"Usually Mr. Nelson isn't able to see anyone without an appointment. He has a very tight schedule. May I ask what this is regarding?"

She was still smiling. I imagined she always smiled. Her skin was like pure cream. I felt like a hunchback just being in the same room as her. I was still glad I wasn't her.

"It's personal," I answered.

"I'm Mr. Nelson's personal secretary," she said. "Surely you can tell me the nature of your inquiry?"

"It's about his daughter."

I was pleasantly surprised when it worked. "Okay then," she said. "Right this way." She stood up and led me through another door, which led down a short hall and into Mr. Nelson's office.

It was, naturally, a corner office. About a thousand feet by a million. So much mahogany you would think you were in a forest. Leather furniture you could probably reach right through with your bare hand. A carpet so plush I could barely tread through it in my high heels.

"Miss Flannigan," the girl said. "Mr. Nelson."

The Mr. Nelson in front of me was almost at middle age, with square shoulders and blond hair streaked with gray, sitting behind a desk the size of a Cadillac. The look on his face told me he was a busy man, and very important, and I'd better not forget it.

I had never seen him before in my life.

"Sit," he said. He gestured to a chair on the other side of the desk and I took it. He didn't smile and he didn't get up. "Now, Miss Flannigan, what's this about my daughter? The police were here earlier today, and they wouldn't tell me anything, either."

"Your daughter is named Nadine?" I asked.

He nodded. "That's her."

"Do you have a picture?"

He frowned and looked at me suspiciously. "What's this all about? Who are you?"

"I'm a private investigator," I told him. "Or rather, I work for one. We have reason to believe your daughter was a witness to a crime—"

"What kind of a crime?" he interrupted.

"Mr. Nelson," I said, as if he had asked the most ridiculous question in the world. "You're a lawyer. I'm sure you understand confidentiality. I only have a few questions. I won't take up too much of your time. Now, you say the police were already here?" I didn't know where I had learned that voice—it was smooth and professional and kind of snaky—but I thought it sounded good.

He nodded. "They were asking me all kinds of questions, but they wouldn't tell me anything. What's this about Nadine being a witness to a crime?"

"I'm not surprised the police were here," I said. But I was. Springer was checking out my story. And I was willing to bet it hadn't checked out good. "I'll need much of the same information you gave them. As a lawyer, I'm sure you know that they're not always able to do their job as well as we'd like. Now, do you have a photograph of Nadine?"

There were three picture frames on his desk, facing him, and I couldn't see them but I guessed that one would be his daughter. I was wrong. Instead he reached into his desk drawer, looked around for a minute, and pulled out a photograph in a silver frame. He handed it to me. It was Nadine, all right. In better days. She wore a white satin gown and held a corsage of white flowers. Some type of debutante party, probably. She was smiling. I realized I had never imagined her smiling.

"Do you know where she is now?" I asked.

He shook his head. "I haven't seen her for months."

"Have you tried looking for her recently?" I asked. "Have you hired anyone to find her?"

He looked at me like I was trying to sell him a gallon of snake oil. "That's what the police asked. I don't know who you are, lady, or what you want, but I never hired anyone to find my daughter. I know who she is, and what she is. I don't know where she is, or if she's alive or dead. And I don't want to know."

I don't know what kind of reaction he expected, but I didn't give him any at all. After a minute he missed the sound of his own voice and he started talking again. "I did everything for her. For all my kids. I've got three. The other two are just fine, thank God. The boy's in medical school and the girl's engaged to a good fellow, going to be a lawyer. But Nadine—she was always a problem. First she started trouble with the family next door, then—"

"What kind of trouble?"

"With the father. He's an old friend of mine, nicest man you ever met. She said he did all kinds of things, crazy things—"

"I understand," I said.

"She's been one headache after another ever since. I sent her to Barnard—do you know what that costs?— and she just got into more trouble, failing her classes, causing all kinds of problems. She never came home anymore—"

"Where do you live, Mr. Nelson?"

"New Village, in Westchester. But I don't know why I'm telling you any of this. It's my own problem, not yours, and I still don't know what the hell you want. I can tell you there's no reward or anything like that for finding my daughter, if that's what you thought. I'm not looking for her."

"Yes, I understand that. But if you wouldn't mind just a few more questions. She never came home anymore . . ."

"Right. Never came home anymore. Had all these new friends, bohemians or whatever you call them, lowlives if you ask me, and they're the ones who got her on drugs. We tried to help her a thousand times, we did everything we could, but she didn't want to stop. Eventually she got herself expelled from school, and then she just took off."

"So when was the last time you saw her?"

"Probably a month before that. Broke her mother's heart."

"And you haven't seen her since?"

He shook his head. "I haven't seen her, and I don't want to. She's not my daughter anymore."

I bought a map at a gas station to find my way to New Village. When I was close by I used a phone book in a drugstore to find the Nelsons' house. I had heard of places like New Village before, but never seen anything like it. Block after block of houses, all exactly the same, like they all sprang up together out of the blue one day. A new car in every driveway. Every house had a little lawn out front, and every blade of grass on each lawn was trimmed down to the exact same height. Some of the ladies had flower beds and even the flowers all looked alike, something small and pink. There wasn't a person out on the streets, which made sense seeing as there were no sidewalks—the lawns came all the way out to the road. It gave me the creeps.

Each street in New Village was named after something lovely: Sunset Drive, Mockingbird Lane, Maple

Leaf Road. The Nelsons lived on Pleasant Avenue. Mrs. Nelson answered her door on the first ring.

"Are you Mrs. Nathaniel Nelson?" I asked.

"Yes, can I help you?" She smiled, but it was thin. She was around forty, slender and pretty with short blond hair in a fancy do, wearing a plain blue dress. I could see the resemblance to Nadine. She had on a full face of makeup. I wondered who would put on that much makeup to sit around her house in New Village all day.

I thought I heard someone talking inside the house. But then I peered in and saw a television set in the living room. I had never seen one, except in the stores. It was amazing, like a miniature movie theater right there in her house, except the picture was small and fuzzy. Two ladies were sitting around a kitchen table. "I don't understand," one woman said to the other. From the look on her face she was pretty torn up. "Bob NEVER finishes his breakfast anymore."

The other woman looked at her wisely. "Have you tried Vita-Crunch?" she said, as serious as if it were a funeral. "You know, nine out of ten doctors recommend Vita-Crunch."

For the second time that day, I felt lucky. At least I didn't live my life putting on makeup to watch cereal commercials all day.

"Yes. I'm here about your daughter, Nadine."

Mrs. Nelson's smile dropped. "Is she okay?"

She didn't say anything about the police. I guessed they probably hadn't bothered with the wife. "I don't know," I said. "That's why I'm here."

"Do you want to come in?"

"No thanks," I said. Like I said, the place gave me the creeps. "I work for a private investigator in New York City, Mrs. Nelson. We have reason to believe your daughter witnessed a crime and we're desperately hoping she can help us. Do you have any idea where she is?"

"No, I— Is Nadine okay?"

"When was the last time you saw her?"

"About a month ago."

"And did you recently hire anyone to find her whereabouts?"

She looked confused and shook her head. "No, I mean . . . it's not like I never see her. Every once in a while I go in the city and meet her somewhere."

"Where?"

She frowned. "A cafeteria, coffee shop—someplace like that. I mean, I can't take her someplace nice. Not looking like she does."

"And what does she look like?"

Mrs. Nelson grimaced. "Skinny, dirty—well, like a whore. Like a drug addict and a street whore," she said angrily. "Do you have children?" she asked.

"No," I told her. "I can't."

She looked at me. There's usually only one reason why a healthy woman can't have children. Maybe a woman like her could find a real doctor when she needed one. But not me.

"I'm sorry," she mumbled. I didn't say anything. "You don't know," she said, more softly. "You don't know . . . to see your own daughter, like *that*."

"You ever try to bring her home?"

Mrs. Nelson shook her head and looked down at the ground. "Oh no, I couldn't do that. She couldn't come back here. Her father . . . He wouldn't like that at all. We couldn't have her around. Not in the state she was in."

"How about her brother and sister?"

She shook her head. "Nadine was never close to them. She's much younger." She tried to make a little smile. "I . . . I had some female problems, too, and I didn't think I could have any more children until Nadine came along."

"The last time you saw her," I asked, "where was she staying?"

Mrs. Nelson shrugged. "She was living with girl-friends, I think. I don't know. Maybe a man. I don't know where she was living then, or how she was supporting herself. Of course I gave her whatever I could, whenever I saw her, but Nathaniel has a budget for me, and there's only so much we can do without. He doesn't want me giving her any money, he's been very firm about that. He doesn't know that I see her at all."

"How did you talk to each other? Did she leave a phone number, or—"

"No," Mrs. Nelson said. "I guess they don't have phones in the kind of places she stays. She's always called me whenever . . . whenever she was desperate enough, I guess."

"How about this neighbor?" I asked. "I heard there was a problem with the man who lived next door?"

Mrs. Nelson looked everywhere except at my face. "I don't know. Nathaniel said it was impossible. That he would never . . . Nadine always was . . . dramatic, I guess you'd call it. She was an artist, you know."

"I know," I said. "I saw one of her drawings. It looked good."

She smiled. "She is good, isn't she?" I smiled back. "You know I always liked to draw, too, but I never had the chance. . . . Well, I was so pleased when Nadine took an interest in it. That's one thing that gives me hope. At least she has something. . . ."

She started to cry, but kept herself under control. That was all she knew. I asked her to be more specific about the places she had met Nadine. She could remember two: a Ukrainian coffee shop on the Lower East Side and a cafeteria near Times Square, but she didn't know their names. There were over a dozen of each. It didn't do me any good.

"Do you think she's okay?" Mrs. Nelson asked before I left.

"Yeah," I lied. "I think she's fine. From what you've told me I think this was all a big misunderstanding. The girl who was mixed up in all this—I don't think it was Nadine at all. I'm sure Nadine's just fine. I'll let you know."

"Really?" she said. "You really think she's okay?"

"I'm sure of it," I said. I made myself smile. "It's just a misunderstanding. Nadine is in no kind of trouble at all."

A relief came over her that was so strong it almost rubbed off on me.

"And who did you say you were working for?" she asked. "I was so startled when you came to the door, I've forgotten what you said."

"I'll be sure to let you know when I find Nadine," I said, and walked back to the car.

Just for good measure, I threw a rock through the window of the house next door before I left New Village.

# Chapter Nineteen

The drive back to the city seemed longer than the drive out. It was just as I'd thought: Nadine's family had no idea where she was and had nothing to do with any of this. It was most likely that Jerry had cut Nadine loose as soon as they got into trouble. The girl in the Royale had said that Nadine was leaving to meet Jerry somewhere later. He probably never showed up. She knew where they had stolen the dope from. That was probably who had killed McFall. And my chance of finding her was about as good as finding the pot of gold at the end of the rainbow. I'd thought I was at a dead end before. I didn't know just how dead an end could be. I wouldn't waste any more time looking for her. There were other ways to find out who McFall had been dealing with.

In the Bronx, up north where it was still the country, I stopped at a gas station to fill up the Rocket 88. And I noticed something funny. Behind me on the road had been a black Chevy, a few years old, a big dusty car that needed a wash—although by now, so did Jim's. I'd noticed it because I was switching lanes a lot, trying to shave a few seconds here and there off the trip. And the black sedan kept right up with me. That wasn't so strange.

But now that same car pulled into the station just behind me. Not over to the pumps, but over by the office, like he was going to get a Coke. Except he didn't get out of the car. I must have passed five gas stations on the way. And there was nothing special about this one.

The kid pumping gas came to my window. "Sorry," I said. "I forgot—I don't have any money on me. I'll come back later."

"Yeah, sure," he spat out, and walked away. I waited a minute. No one got out of the Chevy. I pulled back out and got on the road going south again. The Chevy followed. I kept in the same lane, now, so he could get right up behind me and I could get a look at him in the rearview mirror. But he didn't. He was following me, all right, but he wasn't quite that dumb, and he put a few cars in between us now.

All this time I'd been wondering how someone could

have followed me to McFall's without my noticing. Because I was sure someone had followed me—there was no other way for them to know when I found McFall. But now I saw that it was pretty easy to follow someone. If I hadn't pulled into the gas station, I never would have noticed the Chevy at all.

The Chevy kept up a good pace behind me and at the next gas station I pulled in and let the attendant fill up the car. While he was doing that, the Chevy pulled in, not to one of the pumps, but by the office again.

While the kid was filling up the car I got out and went over to the Chevy. He pulled out of there and back onto the road so fast you'd think I'd pulled a gun on him.

I didn't mind being followed. I wasn't making any secret of where I was going. But I did want to know who he was. It was probably the same person who had followed me to Brooklyn. And if he didn't kill McFall himself, he probably knew who did. There was no one else who would be so interested in how I was spending my time. But he was gone now, and I'd have to wait until next time to try to catch him.

I was sure there would be a next time.


Jim answered his door with a copy of the *Daily News* in his hand, open to the entertainment page.

"Read all about it," he said. I came in and sat on the

sofa and looked at the paper. There was a picture of Shelley. I glanced at the column next to it.

*Lovely lady Shelley Dumere is slated to star in the upcoming weekly television production* Life with Lydia. *The sultry starlet will star opposite Tad Delmont as wacky housewife Lydia Livingston, whose antics and mishaps are sure to keep us laughing all the way until next week. . . .*

"Great," I said. "Listen. I need to talk to you about your car." His face fell. I told him the car was fine. Only I wasn't giving it back quite yet, if he didn't mind, on account of that I might need it, because I was being set up for murder and had a lot of errands to run.

Jim went to the bar and fixed us each a drink in the fancy glasses with the gold seashells, and he stood by the bar while I told him everything that had happened since the last time I saw him.

"So," Jim finally said when I finished. "What are you gonna do?"

It took me a minute to realize what I didn't like about that question. It was the *you*. I was thinking it might have been a *we*. He brought me my drink and then went back by the bar and leaned against it.

I looked at Jim's face. It was like something had drained right out of it. Like he was locking a part of himself up, and he wouldn't let it out again. Not around me.

I didn't blame him. Jim had stuck with me through

some tough times, but this was different. He couldn't afford this kind of trouble. Nobody could.

I shrugged. "I'm gonna find out who killed Jerry McFall."

I looked at Jim. His eyes were on his drink. "If there's anything I can do," he said. "Anything at all . . ."

It was kind of sweet, when you thought about it. He was saying everything he was supposed to say. He just couldn't look me in the eye when he said it. Sometimes it was hard to believe Jim was a professional con man. Because he wasn't a very good liar at all.

"No," I said. "I don't think so."

"I'll see what I can find out," he said. He was looking at the bar now. "Talk to some people. Ask around."

"Sure," I said. "Thanks."

I stood up and told Jim it was time for me to go. I could almost see the relief on his face. Then he looked me in the eyes.

"The car," he said. "It's yours, Joe, for as long as you need it. Keep it. It's the least I can do."

The least he could do. And the most he would.

"You're gonna be okay, Joe," he said when I was leaving.

It was a statement, not a question, and I figured the least I could do was say, "Yeah. I'll be fine."

*    *    *

By the time I got home it was after twelve. I lay in bed and didn't sleep for hours. I tried to stop thinking, but I couldn't.

It was always hard for me to sleep. I still dreamed about dope, sometimes. Dreams where I'd be doing something ordinary, walking down Fifth Avenue or something like that, and then all of a sudden I'd find myself in a dark little room somewhere, one of a thousand dark little rooms I had been in, and the room would be full of people fixing and I would be, too. I'd have my works out and my arm tied off and someone would be cooking up a fat dose of junk in a spoon and I would smell that smell and the next thing I knew I'd be taking a shot.

*Oh no*, I'd think. *No, no, no. Not again. Not anymore.* It would be like all the hard work of the past two years and all the other times I'd tried to quit before that, all the awful cold turkey and the chills and the crying and the grinding my teeth so hard I chipped them, all the horrible willpower that it took and that it still took, every day—it was all for nothing. Because here I was right back in the middle of it again. I'd be so ashamed of myself that I'd start to cry. How could I be so weak again, so stupid again, when I tried so hard and prayed so much?

*No*, I'd think. *Please God, no.*

But then at the same time, I'd also be thinking, *Yes. Please God, yes.*

165

Finally I got out of bed and moved a chair over to the window and watched the sun come up over Second Avenue. No one was out. The city looked like it had been abandoned, like a ghost town. The streets went from black to gray to pink to gold, and then the sky turned lighter and lighter until the sun was out and the sky was blue. Soon a few trucks started rattling around delivering bread and newspapers and milk, and slowly it all came back to life. One at a time the people took their places on the sidewalks again and the cars and buses took their places on the streets, and it was like the quiet of just a few hours before had never happened. Like everything had always been this way, and it always would. And it seemed like the whole city was mine, watching it from up there, and I wanted to hold on to it forever.

# *Chapter Twenty*

The next afternoon I drove down to the Red Rooster. Harry wasn't there, but that was fine, because I knew where he lived. The Prince George on the Bowery rented beds by the night. From what I had heard not only was the desk wrapped in chicken wire, but each bed was, too, to protect each fellow from the man in the bed next to him. That was how Skinny Harry lived.

Like all the others, this Prince hotel used to be better than it was now, but not by too much. On one side of the lobby was a battered wood counter. To the left was a small waiting room, where a handful of old men sat on threadbare furniture. Half of them were on the nod and the other half were drunk. Their shirts were frayed and their hats, if they had them, were crumpled and dirty. Three of them were talking about the races. One of them liked Lucky Lucy for the third tomorrow.

"If I could get a ride to Belmont," he said over and over again, "I could turn this dollar into fifteen. I *know* I could."

I heard a man sobbing from upstairs. The sound echoed down through the lobby. When I was trying to get the attention of the old man behind the counter another man walked in, a respectable-looking man in a black suit. The old man behind the counter sprang to life.

"Oh no, you son of a bitch," he shouted. "I said you're never stepping foot in here again and I meant it."

Without a word the respectable-looking man turned around and left. Then the clerk turned his attention to me.

I told him that I needed to see Harry and I needed to see him now. He shrugged. "I ain't leaving the desk. But you can ask one of the boys to get him for you."

He looked out toward the lobby. The boys. I went up to one of them, a tall heavyset Negro around a hundred years old who looked like there still might be some life left in him. At least enough to go upstairs and get Harry.

"Hey, mister," I said. "You know Skinny Harry? I'll give you a dollar if you go upstairs and get him for me."

He looked at me. And kept looking. I reached into my purse and got a dollar out. "Look," I said. "I really got a dollar. And it's all yours if you go and get my friend."

He kept on looking. I gave him the bill. He took it. Then he smiled, and when he smiled he didn't look like an old Negro in dirty clothes wasting time in the lobby of the Prince George hotel. He looked like someone you'd like to have a cup of coffee with.

"All right," he said. "I'll be back down with Harry before you can spit."

I didn't spit, but Harry came down the stairs fast. I don't know what the old man had told him, but Harry looked happy, like maybe someone had come by with a puppy dog and a ten-dollar hooker for him. But when he saw me his face fell and he rolled his eyes.

"Oh Jesus Christ, Joe. Ain't I done enough for you already?"

I took his arm and led him out to the street before I said anything. The old men ignored us. Outside I turned to face him and he cringed, like he thought I might hit him.

"Yeah, you son of a bitch, you did plenty for me. You got me set up for murdering Jerry McFall."

Harry's face twisted up and he looked at me. "But Jerry ain't dead, Joe. What the hell are you talking about?"

"He is now, you nitwit."

I watched as Harry's face twisted up even more, and then slackened out to something like sadness. He started to speak a few times, but couldn't get a sentence out.

Finally he said, "I can't believe it. Jerry's been kilt."

I nodded. "Yeah," I said, a little more softly. "Jerry's been killed. You didn't know anything about it?"

He shook his head, slowly. "I gotta sit down or something."

He looked pale so we went back inside and sat on two armchairs, near the old men. I gave Harry a few minutes, and then I asked him if he knew anything else about the job Jerry had pulled off right before he died.

He ignored me. "Jesus," he said. "Jerry's dead. I used to do stuff for him—you know, run errands and stuff—and he always took care of me. He always took care of me good. Now . . . don't know what I'm gonna do now."

"You'll be okay," I said.

"I can't work like I used to," he said, shaking his head. "Remember the jobs we used to pull? Like in Buffalo? And then that other time, in Chinatown with Easy Mike?"

"Sure," I said. "I remember."

"Yeah," he said. "I can't do that stuff no more. Not since the war. I fucked up my head." He smacked himself lightly on his forehead with the heel of his hand. "That's why I run errands and stuff like that now. I fucked up my head."

"You'll be okay," I said again. "Jerry treated you pretty good, huh?"

Harry shook his head. "I don't know. Not really. We weren't really friends, like I made it out to be to you and everyone else. I just did things for him, that's all. Sometimes he would call me stupid and stuff like that. But he never stiffed me. Bring this package to this girl, I'll give you a dollar. He always gave me a dollar here, a quarter there. Now I don't know what I'm gonna do."

"Listen, Harry," I said. "I know you're shook up. But I want you to think for a minute. Really think. You're gonna help me find out who killed Jerry. Do you know where he got his dope from?"

Harry shook his head. "I'm thinking, Joe, I really am. But he never told me nothing like that. I'd deliver it to the girls for him, sometimes. But I never went with him to get it. I don't know anything about that."

I took a deep breath. "Okay. How about the job he pulled, the one that made him go hide out in Sunset Park. Do you know anything about that, anything at all?"

Harry thought for a long time. "He never told me stuff like that. The only reason I knew about that at all was because he called me up and asked me to come out to Sunset Park to bring him some things from his apartment. He called me at the Red Rooster—there's no phone here."

"What did he say when he called?" I asked.

Harry thought some more. " 'I was taking some dope off someone's hands and it didn't turn out like I planned,' " he finally said, in a good imitation of Jerry's oily voice. "Of course I knew what that meant. I'm not stupid. He'd torn someone off, and he'd been busted. Then I asked if he was okay, everything like that. He said 'Sure, I'm okay. I'll tell you, Harry, it was all worth it just to stick it to

171

that son of a bitch. You know the type, thinks they're better than everyone else.'"

"Then what happened?"

"Then he asked me to get some stuff from his apartment—just a couple of suits, some underwear, things like that—and bring them out to him in Brooklyn. Which I did."

I showed him the photo of Jerry and Nadine. By now it was getting soft and crumpled around the edges. "How about Nadine? Did you ever meet her?"

Harry looked at the picture and smiled. "Oh, *that* girl. Yeah, she was hanging out with Jerry a lot for a while there. Real nice. Real sweet girl. But when I went out to Sunset Park he was with that other girl. I asked where Nadine was and he said she was more trouble than she was worth, now. That's exactly what he said. 'That girl's more trouble than she's worth, now.'"

That was all Harry knew. I was getting ready to leave when I thought of something. I asked Harry if he still had the key to Jerry's apartment.

"Sure," he said, "right here." He reached into his pocket and took it out. I asked if I could have it.

"I don't know," he said, slowly. "Would this really make us square? I mean once and for all?"

"Harry," I said, "we're really square."

I gave him ten dollars and told him to look out for himself. He gave me the key.

Driving north on the Bowery I saw a black Chevy behind me. I was at a red light and I saw it just a few cars behind me, waiting for the light to change. He was back. I thought about what to do. Did I want to lose him, or did I want to draw him out, find out who it was? If I wanted to confront him, I could just not start driving again when the light changed. At the very least he'd have to go around me, and maybe I could get a look at his face that way. . . .

And then I saw something else. A few cars behind that was another black Chevy. I looked around. There was another, parked around the corner on Fourth Street. I looked up. Across the street, on top of the gate of a parking lot on Bowery and Fourth, was a billboard. There was a drawing of a black Chevy with a family of four inside. A dog was hanging his head out the window. They looked like they were on their way to a picnic.

*Chevrolet,* it said underneath the picture. *America's most POPULAR car!*

# Chapter Twenty-one

Jerry lived in a brownstone turned over to apartments on West Twenty-seventh Street. The lock on the front door was busted and inside the building smelled like boiled chickens. Jerry's place was on the fourth floor in the rear. I looked around to make sure no one was watching and then I let myself in. It was a stupid thing to do and I knew it. The cops were still investigating and they could be around any minute. But if I was quick I should be okay.

His apartment looked like a hurricane had been through it. Either the cops had already been through it or his killer had been looking for the dope, or probably both. The closets and the dressers and the cabinets were emptied onto the floor. The furniture had been turned upside down and sliced up. There was a bedroom and it was the same in there—everything destroyed. I walked around, trying not to disturb anything too much. Being in a dead man's apartment spooked me.

You'd think you'd be able to tell a lot about a person from his apartment, but nothing stood out. The mirror didn't scream "Jerry McFall's mirror!" It was just a plain mirror hung on the back of the bedroom door. The sofa didn't look like something you'd see and say, "Now that's a sofa a pimp would buy." It was just plain furniture. I don't know what I had been hoping to find there. Maybe a big sign with "SO-AND-SO KILLED ME" hung up on the refrigerator.

I looked through the piles of stuff. There were some household items, things you'd find in anyone's apartment—coffee cups, ashtrays, a corkscrew, a can opener. Magazines. Dime novels. Clothes. A cigarette case. Matchbooks. Records. A pillow from the bed that ended up in the living room. In the bedroom, lying on top of the sliced-up mattress, was a little ceramic deer. There were no signs, no clues, no secret messages.

In a pile of junk in the corner of the living room I found his phone book. It was one of those automatic types, where you slide the lever to the letter you want. I slid it to "A," opened it, and broke the lever off so I could flip through. Most of the names meant nothing to me. I could call every one and ask if they knew who killed him. That probably wouldn't go over too well. But I knew some people in there. Harry, after which he wrote *Red Rooster.* Jim was in there. I wasn't surprised. He said he knew him. I looked through the book some more. Lots of girls' names: Hazel, Clara, Nadine.

And Shelley.

I left everything as I found it and went back downstairs.

On the street in front of the building was a police car, with Springer at the wheel. Parked a few cars down from him was a black Chevy.

"Don't even think about running, Joe," Springer said. "You're coming with me."

"I got a call from one of the neighbors that someone was in McFall's place," Springer said in the car. "It's funny, because I was going to come and find you today, anyway. So you saved me a lot of trouble. I got a lot more people who say you were looking for McFall, people who say you've known the man for years. I think it's time we had a talk."

So I went to the station with him to talk. We talked for about ten hours. It was a funny kind of talking, because no matter what I said, he didn't believe me. Instead Springer kept slapping the table with a big phone book and threatening to do the same to me if I didn't come clean. I told him I was coming clean.

"Listen, Joe," he said. "The mayor's getting pretty

pissed off about all the dope on the streets, and we're not taking any shit from the junkies and the dealers anymore. The whole thing's gone too far. Why, you're bothering good people, regular people. Folks can't even walk around Times Square without getting sick just looking at you, bags of bones begging for change and looking for drunks to roll and tourists to rob."

I told him I wasn't using anymore. He called me a liar. I rolled up my sleeves to show him the scars on my arms, as healed up as they'd ever be. I asked for a female officer to give me a strip search. Springer said there were no female officers in his district, and he'd damn well search me himself, but it wouldn't mean anything, because us goddamn junkies were always finding new places to shoot up. He was right about that.

"I'm better off without Jerry McFall," he said, "and I goddamn well know it. But I've got to get this mess cleaned up before it escalates. I don't want a war breaking out on the streets."

I hadn't slept in about twenty hours. I dozed off a few times and Springer woke me up by smacking the back of my head. But not with the phone book.

Then he tried a friendlier approach. "Aside from the dame," he said, "and of course you, Joe, the last person to see McFall alive was old man Harmon. They were seen together at the Happy Hour the evening before Jerry went into hiding in Brooklyn—the night of the eleventh.

177

So what's the angle, Joe? If you're working for Harmon, all you have to do is tell me, and we'll cut a deal."

I knew old man Harmon. Of course, Springer was wrong—he wasn't anywhere near the last. There was me, like he had mentioned, there was Harry, who'd brought him his clothes, the killer, and probably more. But back to Harmon. If he knew anything about McFall, I could count on him to be square with me.

"Come on, Joe," he said, still trying to be friendly. "If Jim got you mixed up in this, all you have to do is tell me. Why take the fall for him?"

I told him I wasn't taking the fall for anyone.

Finally Springer got a phone call that a businessman from Cleveland had been shot over in Pennsylvania Station and they cut me loose. Everyone cares a lot more about a dead businessman from Cleveland than they do about a dead dope pusher from New York.

It was dawn by the time they let me out. I took a taxi back up to Twenty-seventh Street to get Jim's car and then drove home. I smelled like a police station. When I got to my room I washed up and lay down on the bed, just for a minute, before I got dressed.

When I opened my eyes the sun was coming in at a certain angle and I knew it was early in the afternoon. My head was as heavy as a cannonball and I would have been hungry if I hadn't had such an awful taste in my mouth. I looked at the clock on my nightstand. There was just enough time to get to Harmon before I'd have to wait a whole other day.

I could have stayed in bed all day. But I remembered the idea that had come to me in the car—that if I found whoever set me up, I would take care of them myself. That got me up and out of bed and on my way uptown.

# Chapter Twenty-Two

Harmon was an old gentleman, almost as old as Yonah, who'd been using for years. He had a real distinguished look and he made his living slipping into fine restaurants and good hotels and robbing the places blind. He'd take overcoats, hats, silverware, china, anything that wasn't nailed down. People said he had a real education, and used to be some kind of a writer before he got hooked. That must have been before I was born. Every afternoon he had supper at the Westside Cafeteria. Anyone who wanted whatever he had lifted in the past twenty-four hours could come to the Westside and get a good price, like a sale at a grocery store.

The cafeteria was full of thieves and whores and dope fiends, and I knew a good number of them. There in the corner was Kate from Brooklyn and her newest pimp, Gentleman Jack. Kate had a black eye but she still nodded a hello when she saw me. Jack tipped his hat. Nearby were John the Hat and John the Gimp, two old-time dope fiends who'd been using since before the Harrison Act. They both wished me a good evening. They might have known something about McFall, but if I sat down with them my wallet, my watch, and probably my hairpins would be gone in less than a minute. Finally I saw Harmon, in the back near the kitchen.

"Josephine," he said excitedly when he saw me. He was sitting at a table alone in front of a cup of coffee and a bowl of rice pudding. I couldn't remember the last time I'd eaten anything. I got a plate of fried chicken and a dish of rolls from the counter and brought them with me to Harmon's table.

"Josephine," he said in his slow, creaky way. "You look awful. Don't tell me you're back on stuff."

The food looked horrible but I ate it anyway as I talked. I told him I wasn't, but that I was in a bad way. Worse than dope. As quickly as I could I told him why I was there.

"Jerry McFall," he said, nodding his head when I was done. "The coppers came and talked to me yesterday. Or maybe it was the day before. Anyway, I told them everything I knew, which was absolutely nothing. I certainly didn't mention your name. But I'm not surprised that fool is dead. A while back I bought some dope from him and it was so cut with milk sugar it was practically

181

worthless. Of course I beefed about it, even though I was not expecting any kind of compensation. But he said that if I met him at the Happy Hour in a few days, he would make it up to me. He'd give me a paper of pure uncut stuff. You know the Happy Hour, don't you, Josephine? It's an awful lounge down on Forty-second Street. I didn't believe a word of it. But he told me to meet him and, well, I figured it was worth a try. Of course when I found him there, he was with his friends and he gave me the brush-off. I met up with him outside the place, on his way out. Said he hadn't gotten the stuff yet, but maybe tomorrow. Well, tomorrow never came for him. I mean that metaphorically, of course. He went into hiding for a few days, apparently, before he was killed."

I showed him the picture of Nadine. "What about this girl? You ever see her around?"

Harmon shook his head. "I'm afraid I'm too old to chase after females, Josephine, and I just don't notice them like I used to."

"Do you know anything about his connection?" I asked.

Harmon shook his head. But then he stopped and cocked his head. "Well, that idiot did have quite a bit to say about him that night in the Happy Hour. Of course he said the reason he didn't have the stuff for me was that his connection hadn't come through for him. Called him all kinds of names, said he was a liar and a rat and a dirty Jew. Apparently he really loathed the fellow. Or maybe he was just making excuses for his lack of stuff."

I pressed Harmon for details. "I wish I could tell you more, Josephine," he said. "But I really don't know. Oh, Josephine," he said. "Before I forget. The reason I called you over was to see if you knew anyone who might be able to use a pistol. I can't pawn it, it's too hot, and my regular fellow for this sort of thing is up at Rikers, doing ninety days for insulting an officer."

I was about to say no, I didn't know anyone who needed a gun. But then I stopped myself.

What did I think I was going to do when I found out who killed McFall? Talk to them? Pull out a switchblade or a razor? They sure as hell had a gun. They'd used it once already.

I'd been thinking like a little kid. Like a girl. But I couldn't think like that anymore.

I asked Harmon if I could see the pistol. He slipped it to me under the table. It was warm in my hand. I looked down. I didn't know what a good gun was supposed to look like. I'd been around them all my life but never had any interest in them. I'd never fired one before.

It seemed okay. I wasn't sure if I knew how to use it. What was there to know? You just aimed and fired.

I figured I'd find out for sure if I needed it.

"I'll take it," I said.

Harmon nodded. "That's a good pistol. Smith & Wesson. It'll never give you any trouble." He reached into his pocket and took out a handful of bullets and held them out for me under the table. I took them. "It was loaded when I found it, but you keep it empty, Josephine. Never keep a loaded gun around unless you intend to use it," he went on. "That's like that old line from Chekhov; if there's a gun on the wall in the first act, it better go off in the third act."

He wanted fifty bucks. It sounded fair to me. I gave it to him.

When we were done I locked myself in the bathroom and loaded it.

# Chapter Twenty-three

The Happy Hour was on Forty-second, just west of the Square, in between two movie theaters showing French films. A dark room full of characters dressed up to look fine, or what they thought fine looked like, lying about deals they'd never made and boyfriends they'd never had. Half the people there were doped up on something or other, coke or pills or heroin or opium or tea. That was on top of a good drunk, which everyone there had. I'd only been there a few times before, but I felt like I'd spent half my lifetime in places just like it.

I sat up at the bar and looked around the room. I could go around with the picture of McFall. That would be a sure way to get myself kicked out fast. I had to get clever or find someone I knew. I was too exhausted to get clever so I looked around some more. Most of the crowd I had never seen before. Ten years ago I would have known everyone in the room. But somehow it was all the same anyway. It was like the people I knew had all been replaced by younger versions, dropped down in the exact same place. Through the crowd I saw two girls in the corner, whispering to each other. A group of men at the table were talking too loud, telling stories, trying to impress the girls. Nearby were two fellows and a girl sitting hunched over their drinks, talking quickly and softly, probably about the big deal that was right around the corner.

Across the room I finally saw someone I knew. Linda Lee. She was sitting at a table with two other girls. I'd known Linda for years. She'd wanted to be an actress, like Shelley, and when we were young I thought she just might make it. She was pretty enough and wanted it badly enough, but for one reason or another it had never worked out for her. Now she made the kind of movies that no more than a handful of men ever saw. She did photographs, too, magazines and the sets of prints you sent away for from the classified ads. I didn't know what she would do now that she was getting older. She was starting to get lines around her eyes and slight creases around her mouth. Her black hair was a duller shade than it had been—I guess she tinted it to cover gray. She wore a green dress and I could see that her waistline was getting thicker, her breasts starting to sag.

I wondered what would happen to her. Thousands of men around the world had used her picture. None of them had contributed to her pension plan. Those pictures would be around forever, showing a healthy young girl doing all the things a healthy young girl can do better than everyone else. Meanwhile the real Linda would slowly fade away. There was no retirement plan for hustlers and junkies and whores. Most of us wouldn't live long enough to need one, anyway.

The way things were looking, I sure wouldn't.

Linda was happy to see me. We went to a small table in the corner together, where it was quieter. She told me I looked good, and that she was happy to see it. She wondered how long it had been since we'd seen each other. Was it me she'd seen in Howard Johnson's last month? No, it was that redhead, what's her name? Used to go out with Johnny Stick-Up.

After a minute I realized she'd been sniffing cocaine. I told her I hoped she didn't mind if I cut right to the chase, but I was in an awful bind, and I needed to know if she had seen Jerry McFall around here anytime lately.

"Sure," she said excitedly. "Just a few days ago. Hey, did you hear what happened to him? He's dead, someone shot him and no one knows who. Everyone thinks it's someone he ripped off for dope, but no one knows who it was. I'm not surprised he's gone. He was a real son of a bitch. You know, Joey, I knew that piece of shit for years. A long time ago he took some pictures of me—you know, to sell. Well, the pictures came out so awful he couldn't sell 'em anywhere, no matter what body parts they showed. And then just a few weeks ago he tried to sell them back to me! Like I would want that crap! I mean, Jesus, everything I done and he thinks I wanna buy back a couple of pictures where you couldn't even tell my ass from my elbow. Some of these guys, Joe, you ought to—"

I asked if she could tell me everything she remembered, *everything,* about the last time she saw McFall?

"Well, sure," she said. She seemed anxious to help. And the fact that she was high and felt like talking didn't hurt. "It was the night before he disappeared, I guess a few days before he died. Kind of spooky, huh? I mean, to know I was one of the last people to see him alive? I mean, you wonder what happens to a person like that after they die. Someone like him, he's not going upstairs, if you know what I mean—"

I gently brought her back to that night.

"Right, yeah, the last time I saw him. There was nothing special about it. I had a drink with old man Harmon, you know him—he was pissed off because Jerry was gonna give him some dope and now he was getting the brush-off. But you know Harmon, he's always com-

plaining. He's a nice guy and all, don't get me wrong, but he's never had a happy day in his whole life, to hear him tell it—"

"That's Harmon," I said. "So that night, what else happened?"

"Oh, okay. Hmm." She reached into her purse and pulled out a little glass vial of coke. She bent her head down and took a sniff off the end of a fingernail. She shivered as she straightened back out. "Wow, that's good." Then she stared out into the room for a minute, clenching her jaw tight. I waited another minute for it to pass before I tried her again.

"So, Linda. The last night you saw Jerry. Was there anything else about that night? Who was he sitting with?"

This was beginning to seem like a waste of time. Linda was too high to give me the straight story of what had happened. For all I knew there was nothing to tell, anyway. There was no reason to think anything special had happened that night. It wasn't like he knew he'd be dead in a few days.

Linda snapped back to attention. "What's that, Joe? Sorry, I was just thinking about the whole thing, about . . . I don't remember now."

"McFall, Linda. The last time you saw Jerry McFall. Was there anything strange about him that night?"

Linda shook her head. "I don't think so, Joe. He was

sitting up at the bar, having a drink with some of his pals. I don't know who they were. Then he went outside with Harmon, I guess, or that's what Harmon said. Then I saw him later that night—well, that morning really, at this twenty-four-hour coffee joint over in the Square with your sister."

"What?" I thought I hadn't heard her right.

"He was up at the bar," Linda said. "Having a drink with his pals—"

"No," I interrupted. "The last part."

"Well, after the bars closed, I went out for a cup of coffee with a friend of mine. We went to this joint in Times Square that's open all night. It's called Charlie's or something like that, Charlie's or Harry's, some man's name. It's just a little hole in the wall, they just got coffee and burgers and eggs, I don't know why I end up going there so much because the truth is it really isn't any good—"

"And this place," I said firmly, trying to keep her focused. I must not have heard her right. "McFall was there. And who was he with?"

"With your sister, Shelley, like I said. You know, Joe, I don't mean to be nasty or nothing, but your sister, she's pretty full of herself these days. I mean, I'm real happy for her, being on a television show and all, but she could at least say hi. She acted like she didn't even know me."

"Yeah," I said. "I'd better talk to her about that."

So Shelley knew Jerry McFall. She'd said she might have met him once. "Years ago," she'd said.

Right then I felt like just about the biggest dope in the world. And having been set up for killing Jerry McFall was the least of the reasons why.

# Chapter Twenty-four

I didn't sleep too well again that night. My mind kept running over the craziest things. Like the time when I was a little girl and Shelley was just a few years old, and our mother left us alone for the first time. Just the two of us alone in that tiny apartment. When my mother came back, three days later, I put Shelley down in our bed and went outside without saying a word and sat on the stoop and cried and cried and cried. I'd been so scared. The second time I didn't wait. I left Shelley with the lady next door and I went to the market and I begged the grocer for credit. After a few times my credit was no good. But by then I'd wised up how to make money fast.

After a while I gave up on sleeping and got up and looked out the window again. I took out the gun I'd bought from Harmon. I took the bullets out and then put them back in again and took them out again. I held it in my right hand, straight out ahead of me like I was going to fire. It was heavy. I wondered how long I could hold it for. Not long. With the chamber empty I shot up my apartment. *Click*. There went the percolator. *Click*. My coffee mug. *Click*. A bottle of scotch. *Click*. Here's one for you, Springer. *Click*. That's for you, Jerry McFall.

If he wasn't already dead, I could have killed him.

# *Chapter Twenty-five*

Shelley lived in a fine old building near Gramercy Park, the type of place where all your neighbors have to approve you before you move in. How Mike, the guy who paid for Shelley's place, ever sneaked her in I'll never know. It was mostly ladies who lived there. You could tell from the lobby, where everything was perfect and neat as it would have been in a house on East Sixty-seventh Street. Shelley's doorman didn't mind me waiting in the lobby for her, or at least he didn't mind at first. After five or six hours, he started dropping hints that I might be more comfortable elsewhere. He would even call me when she got there. The doorman was a fellow of about forty who had Brooklyn written all over him, no matter how fancy his uniform was and what kind of airs he put on.

Finally I looked right at him and started to cry. I

don't know how I did it, because I've never been able to cry on purpose before. But I just willed myself to start crying and I did.

"Oh, Chr— Oh, I'm sorry," he said. He started to look frantic, looking around for a tissue or a clean handkerchief or maybe a lollipop to give me.

"It's just—" I let out in between sobs. "There's been an emergency in Miss Dumere's family—" I broke off and started crying again before I could continue. "I really need to speak to her the instant she gets in, the very minute—"

"Oh, I'm sorry, lady," he said again. Finally he found a clean handkerchief in his desk and handed it to me. I cleaned myself up a bit and then squeezed the handkerchief like it was a life preserver. "I'm so sorry I said anything," he sputtered. "I didn't mean—"

"Oh, it's all right," I said. "I know I must be in your way here." He apologized a few hundred more times and then left me alone, and after a few more minutes I made myself stop crying.

Shelley came in at a little after nine. She was wearing a white spring dress, just a plain cotton sundress, but it fit her so snugly and looked so nice I knew it had cost a fortune. She was carrying an armload of shopping bags from different stores, which she dumped at the doorman's feet without even a word. I guess he was supposed to carry them upstairs for her.

195

Then she saw me. She didn't try to cover up her disappointment. "Joey," she said, flatly. "What a surprise."

I stood up. "Hi, Shelley. Can I come up? I need—"

She cut me off. "I'm happy to see you, Joe, I really am. It's just that Jake is supposed to come by any minute now, and he doesn't like it so much when I have girlfriends over." I didn't know who Jake was. I thought the guy who paid for the apartment was named Mike. This must have been a new one. But I didn't care.

Without ever talking about it, Shelley and me had made kind of a deal. I wasn't her sister anymore. Not in public, at least. She was going places and me . . . well, I'd been places, and far too many of them. For me to be here now was making her angry. I could see it on her face. What if one of the neighbors saw us, me in my cheap suit and nylon stockings? What if Jake or Mike or whoever it was came by? He probably didn't even know Shelley had a sister.

I had always stuck by my end of the deal. But this was different. I glanced over at the doorman. He was busy helping some old broad into a taxi. "You take me upstairs right now," I hissed to Shelley under my breath. "Or I swear to God I'll call up every fat old lady in this building and tell them you're a goddamned whore. I'll get you thrown out of this place faster than you can blink."

She turned around and without a word we walked

into the elevator and went up to her apartment. When you walked into Shelley's place everything was white. There were white marble tables and a white velvet sofa and little white chairs that you couldn't sit in and white china and even the bar glasses had white flowers painted on them.

We sat down on the white sofa. She glared at me. I didn't think she'd ever been so angry at me before. "Look," I said. "You're gonna tell me everything you know about Jerry McFall. And don't try telling me that you didn't know the guy, not now."

Shelley looked astonished. She really was a good actress, after all. "Joey, I have no idea what you're talking about. Really, I—"

I felt bad for Shelley. I really did. Our mother was a good-for-nothing drunk, a drunk and a whore. We didn't have the same father, at least we thought we didn't, because neither of us knew who our father was. And she ended up with a worthless junkie as an older sister. Life's tough for some people, and for Shelley it was tougher than most. But I didn't have time to worry about that now. She'd lied to me, and that was fine, but now I needed to know the truth.

I did something then that I'd never done before. I hurt her. I grabbed her arm and turned it around, not hard enough to really cause pain but enough to give her a taste.

"Okay!" she finally said. "All right, I'll tell you."

I let go and she grabbed her arm and started rubbing it, as if it still hurt. Her face fell and she didn't look angry anymore, just tired and maybe ashamed of herself. "I heard about what happened," she said softly. "About him getting shot and everything. Guess that screwed everything up for you, huh? I mean, there's no way for you to find that girl now."

"I don't know, Shell," I said. All the steam had gone out of me. I couldn't stay mad at her. "I'd like to. But I'm not really worried about her right now."

Shelley looked at me with her eyes wide. "You didn't have nothing to do with him getting killed, did you?"

I'd always tried to protect Shelley, even though I had never done a very good job of it. But I would protect her from this if it was the last thing I did. There was no way Shelley was getting mixed up in this. I swallowed hard, and hoped I was a better liar than Jim. "No, of course not. I just need to know."

"I knew McFall," she said quietly. "I used to buy junk from him once in a while. Save your damn lectures—I don't need them. I know it was stupid, but sometimes . . . I don't know. I got bored, I guess. Usually I met him at this little coffee shop in Times Square so no one I knew would see me. I mean, *my* kind of crowd—they never go around there."

"Jesus, Shelley." I was going to say more, but I didn't know what to say.

"I know," she said. She put her head in her hands and laughed the way you do when nothing's funny at all. "I've always been the smart one, huh? Jeez, what a ninny. I don't know why I do it. I don't know why I do half the things I do really—it's like I can't help myself." She laughed again. "Hey, did you hear? I got the part, the part on the television show."

I smiled. "Yeah, of course I heard. I'm proud of you."

She looked down. "Yeah, well, you wouldn't be if you knew how I got it." She sat up and looked at me. "Want a drink?"

"Sure," I said. "Scotch is good."

She went to the kitchen. I picked up a business card off the coffee table. Jake Russo, Real Estate.

She came back with a water glass full of scotch for each of us. "This him?" I asked. "The guy who pays for the apartment?"

She nodded. "Cheap bastard," she said. But she said it softly, like her heart wasn't in it. "He doesn't even pay for this place, you know. He's in real estate, rents out places all over Manhattan. He just fixed the books a little and he doesn't have to pay for this place at all." She looked down at the floor. "I'm sorry I didn't tell you, Joe. About McFall. I wanted to help, I really did. I just didn't want you to know how stupid I'd been, that's all."

"It's okay," I said. "It doesn't matter. You can tell me now. Do you know the girl, Nadine?"

Shelley shrugged. "I dunno. I might have met her with McFall before. She was one of his girls, right?"

I nodded. "Do you know where McFall got his dope from?"

She took a long drink of her scotch. "I really don't know, Joey, honest. But I did go to a buy with him once."

I nearly hit the roof. "So you do—"

"No," she said. "I didn't see who it was. What happened was, I was supposed to meet him at that place in Times Square. You know, to get dope. So I get there, and he's got nothing. He buys me a cup of coffee and then after an hour or so, he says he'll be right back. Well, after a while, he's not back, and I've already given him my money, so I go outside to look for him. He's just getting out of a car. So we go back to his place, he cuts the stuff, bags it up, and gives me a few papers."

"But you never saw who it was?" I asked.

Shelley shook her head. "All I saw was the car," she said. "A brand-new Rocket 88."

# Chapter Twenty-six

Gramercy Park was a private park with a locked gate, and inside it looked like something from a movie, even at night; the flowers were starting to come out and the plants were starting to grow and you could tell that every little thing, the plants and the flowers and the trees and the benches, had been placed *just so,* probably by a staff of full-time gardeners. I walked by it on the way home. Just a few blocks south and east there was another park, if you wanted to be generous, because a better word would probably be a *square* or a *plaza.* There wasn't much grass and only a few trees, with a lot of concrete in between. I'm sure it had a name but I didn't know what it was, and I doubted anyone else did, either. There was a hospital with a mental ward nearby, and newly released patients were the only people who enjoyed the landscaping. This was the side of town I lived on, and this was the side of town I always would live on.

When I got to the Sweedmore, Jim was waiting for me in the lobby. He was sitting on the one chair Lavinia had put out; it was a small old-lady chair with faded black velvet padding, covered in dust and as uncomfortable as a straitjacket. I was surprised to see Jim on something so dirty. It might mess up his suit.

He stood up when he saw me come in. "Joey," he said. "I was worried about you. How's it going?"

I told Jim it wasn't looking too good.

"Come on," he said. "Let me buy you dinner."

It was close to midnight. It was too late for dinner. But I said that would be fine. We walked west on Twenty-second Street without talking. I didn't know where we were going but it didn't matter. Any direction was fine.

We were on Twenty-second between Third and Lexington. It was always a quiet block and it was especially quiet now. All the neat little houses had their doors shut and their curtains down. No one was around. We turned north onto Lexington. All the shops were closed for the night, the small, sad little stores no one ever seemed to go into: the Italian cheese shop and the wig maker's and the radio repair shop and the breakfast counter that served awful breakfasts. We made a left onto Twenty-third. Everything here was closed, too, the store for nurses' uniforms and the art supply store and the bank and the florist's and the grocery. No one was around. It was a wide street and it seemed like a waste—all that space and no one there but me and Jim. All that space to ourselves.

"Find anything out?" Jim asked.

"Nah," I said. "Not really. Nothing I didn't already know."

We walked down the street quietly again, Jim in his perfect suit from Orchard Street and his new hat from Belton's. Just like he always wore.

"You want to go to Lenny's? I think he'll still be open."

"Sure," I said. "That'll be fine."

"I've been thinking," Jim said as we walked. "Maybe this wasn't about the drugs, after all. I mean, I'm sure plenty of people had reason to kill McFall. One of the girls, maybe, or one of their parents—"

"I talked to Shelley," I said.

Jim stopped and looked at me.

Sometimes, if you've been unlucky enough to find out the truth, you're better off forgetting it. Especially when there's not much you can do with it. It was unlikely that anyone would believe me. I'd probably just go to jail for twice as long, for two murders. Or maybe get the chair twice. All I'd be getting was revenge. And what if the law did believe me? What did I have to fight for, anyway? Another thirty years of running from the law and trying to stay off dope and never having enough dough for much more than a good meal—it didn't seem worth trying too hard to keep. I could go to Springer, tell him to write down whatever the hell he wanted, and be done with it. At least that way I'd have three hot meals a day and a cot to sleep on at night for the rest of my life. That was more than I could say now. He'd be doing me a favor, when you looked at it like that. Maybe I should just try to take it like a man, take my medicine and go down with dignity and not take it personally.

But I couldn't.

"Joey," Jim said. "I've been thinking. About Shelley. I don't know, Joe, I hate to say it, but I'm not sure if you should trust her as much as you do."

I looked around. No one was coming our way. I couldn't see another person anywhere. It was as if the whole city had cleared out and left just us, just us two poor dumb schmucks here on Twenty-third Street left to work everything out for ourselves.

It wasn't just what Shelley had said about the car. That was just the icing on the cake. There were lots of little things like that. His number being in Jerry's book. What Harry had said Jerry told him: *I'll tell you, Harry, it was all worth it just to stick it to that son of a bitch. You know the type, thinks they're better than everyone else.* The girl at the Royale said almost the same thing: *Guess the guy thought he was really someone, thought he was better than Jerry. It really burned him up.* Harmon had McFall saying his connection was a "dirty Jew." That could have been a lot of people—but maybe not. As far as I knew there weren't too many Jewish fellows, with heroin connections and a reputation for being full of themselves, who knew Jerry McFall, driving around in Rocket 88s. But there could have been more than one.

There was the fact that Jim was the only person I knew who could pull off a con so perfectly, who would even think of sending in shills and doing it so cleverly. There was the fact that Jim had given me so many good leads, been so interested in helping me. He'd sent me to Paul's, sent me to Bryant Park. He was the only person who knew I was going to Brooklyn that night. And there was the way Jim didn't lift a goddamned finger to help me once he knew I was in trouble.

But that didn't prove anything, either. It could have all been coincidence. Jim happened to work with a con man, he happened to be full of good ideas on how to find McFall, he happened to know where I was going that night, and then he happened to lose interest in me all of a sudden. It was possible.

None of that mattered. I knew it was Jim because it couldn't have been anyone else. There was no one else in the world who knew me well enough to set me up just like this. That was why I had known it was Jim from the very beginning. I had spent the past three days trying to prove it wasn't so. But I couldn't, because it was so. It was just like this.

I had the gun I'd bought from Harmon in my purse, and I wrapped my hand around it while we kept walking, while Jim was saying why it wasn't really about the drugs, after all. Then I stopped and pulled the gun out of my purse and held it in both hands. I pointed it at Jim.

"Jesus, Joe," he said softly. "What the fuck are you doing?"

He took a step toward me.

"Stop," I said. He stopped.

"All right," Jim said, "I'll do whatever you say. Just take it easy."

"I am taking it easy," I said. "I'm taking it very easy. Why me, Jim? What the hell did I ever do to you?"

"Joey," he said. "I don't know what you're talking about." He looked at me like he was looking at a crazy woman. "Joey. Come on. What did Shelley tell you?"

We circled each other on the dark street. There were no sounds except a faraway car rumbling down Third Avenue.

"Who was the man in the Chevy, Jim? Does he work for you, or do you work for him? Which one of you killed McFall?"

Jim didn't answer me. He just kept looking at me.

He took a step closer.

"Don't, Jim. I'll kill you."

He stood still and looked at me.

"Why me, Jim? If you were in a bind I would have helped you out of it. You should have told me, Jim. You didn't have to do this."

"Joey," he said, slowly. "You're exhausted, that's all. You're not thinking clearly. Come back to my place with me, take it easy for a while—"

"Shut up!" I said. Sweat was running down my forehead and into my eyes. I took one hand off the gun to wipe my eyes clean. When I opened them Jim's hand was in his coat pocket. He quickly pulled it out. I knew what was in that pocket. A gun. Probably bigger than mine. And I was sure he knew how to use it. He'd shot plenty of people in the war, and probably some before. And at least one afterward.

"Joey," he said. He said my name like nothing had changed. Like we were friends again.

"Jim."

He wasn't going to tell me anything. It was time. I felt like I was floating. I was seeing everything from a strange angle I had never seen from before. It all looked different from up here. Simpler. I was glad to be up here, floating all above it. I wouldn't have wanted to be on the ground, right there in the thick of it.

Except that I wanted to kill him.

I pulled back the hammer on the gun and aimed it

at his chest the best I could. He pulled his arm up and straightened it out, and in the dark I saw a flash of shiny metal.

I had my finger on the trigger and I heard an awful shot and Jim went down. He fell back and landed on the sidewalk with a heavy thud, bouncing a little before he lay flat. Bits of him flew around and blood sprayed out in every direction.

But it wasn't possible. I hadn't fired.

I hadn't killed him. Someone else had.

The streets swayed to the right and then to the left, and back and forth a few times before they evened themselves out. I tasted something awful in my mouth. My dress was soaked in sweat. I thought I would throw it out when I got home.

I looked around. A flashlight was shining in my eyes. I blinked a few times. It was coming from across the street. I heard someone say, "He's down now, Joe. We got him good." I was sure it was a voice I knew, and knew well. But I couldn't place it. "You're lucky we were here," I heard. "Your aim was way off, you would have missed him by a mile."

He turned the flashlight down and I could see his face. Detective Springer.

Springer and his thug came out from the shadows across the street. We all walked over to Jim, who lay on the ground where he had stood ten seconds before. He'd been shot above his stomach and below his heart, and his suit was torn up and stained red. Blood poured out from his back and made a pool around him. The bullet had gone clean through him. He had a grimace on his face. I guess the last few seconds had hurt like hell. A pistol was in his hand, ready to fire.

I wished none of this had happened. I closed my eyes again and thought maybe none of it really had.

The two cops poked him around a little, made sure he was nice and dead. Then I heard sirens, and four squad cars rolled around with about a dozen officers inside. They got out of the car and drew their guns and began swarming around the street toward me. Sergeant Springer started yelling, ordering everyone around. A couple of the guys yanked me toward their car, searched every inch of me, and then threw me in the backseat and took me over to the precinct, lights flashing all the way.

# Chapter Twenty-seven

At the precinct two young good-looking fellows in suits locked themselves in a room with me and asked me about a thousand questions over a metal table, which they slapped their hands on a lot. I was kind of in shock and it was hard to listen to their questions. Then they asked about a thousand more, and I began to wake up. I began to realize they weren't asking me the questions they should have been. They weren't asking why I was going to shoot Jim. They were asking why Jim killed McFall.

Finally I started asking questions back. Like how did they know about Jim and McFall?

"Shut up," one of them said. "You're looking at getting the chair for shooting Jerry McFall. We'll ask the questions and you'll answer 'em."

I didn't think I would get the chair for shooting McFall, but I shut up anyway. Finally Springer came in the room, with a big smile on his face, and sat down next to me. The two good-looking boys smiled along with him.

"Good work, Joe," Springer said. "You helped me nail someone I've had my eye on for ten years now. We ought to put you on the payroll."

The good-looking boys laughed. I didn't. "How'd you know?" I said. "How'd you know Jim killed McFall?"

"You understand," Springer said, "I don't give a shit who killed Jerry McFall. When you people shoot each other, it's like you're doing me a favor. You know that."

I knew that.

"But there's too many people pushing junk in this city now. It's in the goddamn *Times* practically every day. People are getting scared. So I'm getting pressure from above to make arrests. When McFall turns up dead, I know he's selling dope, so I think maybe it was his connection, some kind of a lovers' quarrel." He laughed at his own joke. "Yeah, a lovers' quarrel. Because the thing is, Joe—you might be interested in this, actually—we're gonna be taking a new approach to all this. The mayor, he doesn't want us to just pick up the street dealers anymore. He wants us to go after the big fish, the dealers who sell to all the guys who sell on the street. So when McFall gets killed, I figure maybe it's his connection. A big fish. And then when I get back from the scene I get a phone call. There's a man on the phone, telling me I ought to look into Josephine Flannigan for the Jerry McFall case. I didn't know it then, but of course that was your friend Jim Cohen on the phone. Your sweetheart or whatever you call it at your age."

Springer laughed, and the good-looking boys laughed along with him. "Anyway," Springer went on. "I start asking around, and I find out you've been asking around. Now I've known you since you were a kid, Joe, and I never had you pegged as a killer. Everything else, maybe, but not to kill a man, not for money. Maybe if it was a crime of passion or something like that, but not over money. So I figured either you had something going on with this McFall yourself, or someone was trying to set you up. And that's what it was, huh? Someone trying to set you up. Anyway, I figured you'd get to the bottom of it fast enough, especially if you figured your life was on the line. If you thought I was falling for the setup. So we had a man follow you for a couple days, and you led us right to him. Jim Cohen. I've had my eye on him for a long time. When the stuff started flooding the streets again, I had him pegged for it right away. And it looks like I was right."

"You've had someone following me?" I asked. It was all sinking in slowly, one word at a time. "You've been following me this whole time?"

Springer smiled. "That's right, Joe. Surprised you didn't notice it." He tapped his hand on the table.

"Of course," I said, mostly to myself. "The black Chevy."

"Well, I don't know what kind of a car Reynolds was driving," Springer said. "We got a whole fleet of 'em for undercover work. All I know is that now we've got a major supplier down, which is gonna make my captain mighty happy. Plus we've got McFall's murder tied up, not that I gave much of a shit, but it's always nice to close a case."

"You knew I didn't do it?" I said. "Jim could have killed me back there. I thought I was going away for life."

"Take it easy, Joe," Springer said.

"Take it easy!" I said, standing up. My hands started to shake. "For three days now I've been thinking I was going upstate for killing McFall, Jim is dead, and I almost got killed myself, you goddamn—"

That was it for Springer. He stood up and backhanded me across the mouth, hard enough that I fell on the floor. Then he sat back down again. The good-looking boys laughed again. I didn't. After a minute I reached over to my chair and pulled myself up into it. My hand was skinned from trying to stop the fall and my ass was bruised from my hand not doing the job.

"Okay," I said. My lip was swollen and I tasted blood. "Okay."

"I don't want any more bullshit out of you, Joe," Springer said. "I could let this whole thing go and let you take the fall for Cohen and McFall. Don't forget it."

"Okay," I mumbled through my swollen lip. "I know. I won't forget it. But can I ask you something?"

"Sure." Springer smiled. I guess he always felt good after smacking a woman. "Go ahead."

"Whatever happened to the girl? Nadine?"

Springer shrugged. "I don't know. Her parents weren't interested so I let it go. Her father said she's a junkie and a whore and they don't want nothing to do with her anymore."

"So where is she now?" I asked.

"I don't know and I don't care," Springer said, smiling again. "I guess she ended up wherever girls like that go. You'd know better than me, huh?"

"Yeah," I said. "I guess I would."

# Chapter Twenty-eight

Shelley was waiting by the door of the Sweedmore when I got home. I was surprised she knew where I lived—she'd never been by before. She was wearing a white suit and had a white scarf wrapped around her head and white gloves and a big white purse and dark glasses, with white rims, like a movie star. She looked pretty, but too pretty, like she was wearing a costume, and she seemed nervous, looking down at the ground and shuffling her feet a little, like she was shy. Maybe she thought I didn't want to see her.

"Hey," I said. "How's it going?"

"Okay," she said. She looked up. "I saw in the papers. About Jim and everything."

"The papers?"

"Sure," she said. "The morning edition."

I realized I'd been in the police station all night. Then I understood why Shelley had come.

"You don't have to worry," I told her. "I mean, about me doing anything like I said I would—telling the people in your building or anything like that. If I was in the papers—"

"No," she said quickly. "I ain't worried about that. I mean, *I'm not* worried. They didn't even print your name. Just that there was a big shootout in Manhattan. A big drug dealer got killed. I had to kind of read between the lines to figure out what happened. Besides, even if they did, no one would know, right? I mean, I'm Shelley Dumere now."

"Right," I said. "So. You wanna get a cup of coffee or something?"

She looked around, and then looked back down at the ground. "Nah, I got to get to work. We're starting rehearsals for the TV show today." She smiled. "I was just . . . I just wanted to come by and tell you . . . you know, that I was sorry how it all turned out. I kind of . . ." She fidgeted with her hands a little, taking one in the other and squeezing it. "I kind of felt bad for not helping you out. For not telling you what I knew about McFall and everything when you first asked. Maybe things could have turned out different."

"It's okay," I said. There wasn't much else to say.

"Anyway," Shelley said. "I guess it's all over now. I mean, Jim's dead. And the girl, Nadine—she turned out not to have anything to do with it all, right?"

I thought about it for a minute. I had enough money left to live on for a few months. I didn't have any reason to work. I didn't have any reason to do anything, really. "I guess I'll find her anyway."

Shelley took off her sunglasses and looked at me. "Why?"

I didn't say anything.

"She might not even be alive," Shelley said. "I mean, you know what happens—"

"Either way," I said. "I guess I'll find her."

Shelley looked around again, and didn't say anything for a minute. Then she looked at me. "If you find her," she said, "if you find Nadine, what are you gonna do with her?"

I shrugged.

"Her parents don't want her, right?"

"No. They don't want anything to do with her."

"Well," Shelley said, "she's gonna need a place to stay and money and all that."

"I guess," I said.

Shelley started fidgeting with her hands again. "I know you don't have so much—I mean, no offense or nothing. But, well, maybe you could let me know.

Maybe you could let me know when you find her. If she needs money or a place to stay or anything like that. Or if you do. If you need anything."

"Yeah," I said. "I'll do that."

We stood there for a minute. Neither of us said anything.

"Well, I ought to—"

Suddenly Shelley reached out and took my hand. "I'm sorry," she said. "I really am, Joe. I'm so sorry I didn't tell you the truth."

"It's okay," I said. I squeezed her hand. "Really, it's okay."

She swallowed and I thought she might cry. "You'll call me, right? When you find the girl? You'll call me?"

"Yeah," I said. "I promise. I'll call."

# Chapter Twenty-nine

went down to Allen Street and over to Third Avenue with her photo. The funny thing about street whores is how much they want to help. Every one took a good long look at her photo, and a few said they might have maybe seen her somewhere before—poor invisible Nadine—and that they'd keep their eyes open. And they meant it, too. But the other thing about whores is, they don't keep their eyes open. They can't. If they did, they'd see all the worst of the world. So I gave them all my phone number but I kept asking, on Allen, on Third, on the West Side Piers, even spots I knew out in Brooklyn, over the Williamsburg Bridge.

The day after Jim's funeral Yonah came to see me. We went out for a walk to the square by my house where the mental patients got their fresh air. He said that Gary, Jim's boss, had paid for a big funeral for Jim, and that everyone came: every con man, every hustler, every thief. People came from all over the country.

"Nobody blames you, doll," he said. Yonah looked old and sad, wearing a worn suit and a frayed straw hat. It was summer now and the sun was bright and hot. We walked around the square. "He shouldn't have done that to you. Everyone was saying that. You were always a stand-up girl. You always been right, and everyone knows it. We all went to the funeral, out of respect and all, but Jim was a bum. I mean, to do that to anyone, but his own girl . . ." Yonah shook his head. "His own girl. No one had any idea he was mixed up in dope again. Everyone feels real bad about what happened to you. Some of the guys, Gary and some of the other fellows, they were talking about taking up a collection for you. Or maybe giving you whatever they got when they sold off his stuff."

"Nah," I said. "It's nice of them, but I don't need it."

"You sure?" Yonah said. "They want to do it. Gary, he thought he ought to take care of you, the way he would any fellow's widow."

I shook my head. I didn't want anything from Jim.

We stopped and sat on a bench. Yonah looked at me. "How about you, Joe? You doin' okay?"

"Sure," I said. "I'm okay."

"You couldn't have known," Yonah said. "It wasn't your fault at all, none of it. You know that, don'tcha?"

"I really thought—" I said. "I mean, I really thought Jim—"

I started to cry.

Yonah wrapped his big arms around me, and we sat in the park like that until it was time for him to go back home for his medicine.

I kept looking for Nadine. Finally, on Twenty-seventh and Tenth, on my third trip there, I found a girl I knew from the old neighborhood, Laura, who had seen her. Laura had always been the pretty one on Fifty-third Street. She had curly blond hair and a perfect figure and bright blue eyes. Now she didn't look so pretty. She looked like a dress that used to be nice, but then someone wore it too much and left it in the corner crumpled and forgot all about it.

She was ashamed of herself, and when she saw me coming she turned away and put a hand over her face. I took her in my arms.

"You look great, Laura," I told her, because I didn't know what else to say.

"No I don't," she said. She smiled anyway. "It's good to see you, Joe." But she was looking around the block, shaking a little, and I figured if she didn't get back to work soon she'd get a beating later. I took out Nadine's picture and showed it to her.

Laura smiled. "Sure, I know her. Sweet girl. Real sweet. She used to work out here. What happened to her?"

"I don't know. What do you know about her?"

"Jeez. She used to work for Jesse, like me, for a while." I knew Jesse. He was Laura's pimp. "But she got bad, real bad. With the dope, I mean. She couldn't keep it under control. Any trick came along with a little dope, she'd give it to him for free. Sometimes she'd take off with a guy for days. Jesse beat the hell out of her, a couple of times, but it didn't do anything. She didn't change. Finally Jesse just cut her loose. Now she can't work around here no more. Jesse'd whip her ass till the skin came off if he saw her out here."

"So where do you think she is?" I asked.

Laura shrugged. "You could always try Jezebel's. I mean, where else is a girl like that gonna go?"

# Chapter Thirty

The building was a four-story tenement like a million others in Manhattan. I opened the door and went inside. No locks. No one needed them here. It was a building no one had ever loved. The paint had always been gray and the floor had always been cheap scuffed linoleum. Fat old Jezebel was sitting at a little desk right inside the hallway, just like she always was. Her hair was thinner but it was pulled up in the same tight bun, dyed a dark black. Her fat face hung lower but the small mean eyes were the same. Even the shabby black dress was the same, or could have been.

Jezebel's was a place girls go when they're tired of hustling and tired of trying and tired of being pretty and tired of scoring and just plain tired, exhausted and beat. No one's looking for the girls at Jezebel's. No one wants them. Maybe once they had families and friends and fellows, but not anymore. To the rest of the world they're dead already. It's only them that can't see it. It's only the girls themselves who think that somehow, in some way, they still matter. That they're still alive.

You never see any money, if you're a girl at Jezebel's, and that's how you want it. Jezebel comes to your room three times a day and gives you a shot. If she can, she'll shoot you in the foot, so stockings with garters can cover up your sores. If the veins in your feet are no good she'll just do it wherever she can and charge the tricks less. There's a kitchen downstairs with food whenever you want it. Usually no one wants it. A few times a day a girl stumbles in, in a nightgown or a house robe, and eats a few bites of tapioca or vanilla pudding. But you don't need a lot of nourishment to lie in bed all day. The customers who come to Jezebel's don't expect anything else. That's why the girls like it. No "I wish all the guys were as handsome as you," no "What kind of work do you do, Mr. Smith?" That's for places like Rose's or the Royale. In Jezebel's the girls just lie around all day until they can't take it anymore, and then the ambulance or the coroner's truck comes. No one was locked in. The girls could leave anytime they wanted. They didn't.

I figured I could get in and out of there quick, with or without the girl. Jezebel didn't want any trouble and she didn't want any girls anyone else was looking for.

She looked up at me sharply. She didn't recognize

me. I didn't expect her to. Probably ten girls a month came in and out of Jezebel's.

"What do you want?" she said. Her voice was flat and empty—a voice with no voice in it at all. "Well? What?"

I took the picture of Nadine out of my purse and showed it to Jezebel. "Her."

She looked at the picture for a minute and then back up at me. "What do you want with her?"

"I'm here to take her home."

Jezebel looked at me for another long minute. Then she stood up and began walking down the hall. I followed. At the end of the hall was a staircase. We didn't go up. We went down, to a dark basement with concrete walls. Bare bulbs hung from the ceiling here and there, giving off just enough light to get the general idea of the place. A few dozen clotheslines were strung around the room from wall to wall. Hanging from them were old sheets, making little nooks of almost-privacy. We walked through the maze of curtains to the back of the room. You could see the curtains rustling and hear the ugly sounds coming from behind. Some of the curtains didn't reach the floor and you could see a foot or a hand hanging off a bed. I tried not to look. I had seen it before, and I didn't need to see it again.

When we reached the wall Jezebel stopped in front of the last curtained-off nook.

"She's in there," she said. "You want to go in, or you want to wait till he's done?"

I realized the curtain was rustling and a cot was squeaking on the other side.

"I'll wait," I said. Over a few minutes the squeaking got louder and faster and then stopped. I turned my head. I didn't want to see who was coming out. After a minute I heard the curtain rustle and footsteps walk away.

"Go ahead," Jezebel said. I would have knocked, but there was nothing to knock on, so I opened the curtain and went in.

Nadine Nelson lay on the bed, staring at the wall. She hadn't bothered to dress or to undress; she wore a yellow satin robe with a Chinese pattern, hanging open from her shoulders, covering her arms. Her hip bones stuck out and her ribs were plain enough to count. She didn't wear anything else.

She glanced at us, and then away, stopping her eyes on the filthy curtain across from her.

"She got any clothes?" I asked Jezebel.

"I can find some," she said. Before Jezebel walked away I took a twenty out of my purse and handed it to her. "She'll need dope, too," I said. She nodded and left.

Nadine looked at me, and then back at her favorite stain on the curtain. Her hair was down loose and it was dull and stringy. It hadn't been washed in days, maybe weeks. Her face was covered with a sheen of grease and spotted with pimples.

Jezebel came back with a ratty white summer dress and a pair of worn-out brown mules. She tossed them on the bed, on top of Nadine.

"Put them on," I told her. Slowly she sat up, and took off the robe, showing arms covered with track marks and sores. Slowly, as if she were lifting a hundred pounds, she pulled the dress over her head and slipped the shoes onto her feet. The dress didn't cover up her arms enough. I took off my jacket and eased her arms into it. It was like picking up a doll. She didn't help and she didn't resist.

Jezebel reached into a pocket of her dress and pulled out a handful of papers. I didn't count them. I figured whatever she gave me was the best I was getting out of her. I took them and put them in my purse. Nadine followed the papers with her eyes, and for the first time I saw an expression on her face. Hunger.

"Come on," I said to Nadine. "We're going." She stood up slowly, wobbling a little. I took her arm with my hand, to balance her, and we walked out.

We were halfway to my apartment when I realized Nadine had no idea who I was or where we were going. So I told her the whole story. About how someone hired me and I thought it was her parents and it wasn't, and how I got framed for murder, and how it turned out to be Jim, and he was dead now and this was his car, which was mine now.

"So?" she said at the end. It was the first time she had spoken. Her voice was small and young.

"What do you mean?" I said. We were on my block. I saw an empty spot across the street and I parked the car.

It started to rain, big warm drops of summer rain.

"So what about me?" she said, with a little bit of a whine. "I mean, no one was looking for me after all. Nobody wanted you to find me. So what'd you come and get me for?"

"I don't know," I said.

We sat in the car and watched the rain.

"Am I coming home with you?" she asked.

"I guess," I said. "You have anywhere else to go?"

She shook her head.

"What am I gonna do?" she said after a minute.

The first thing she was gonna do was take a bath, because she was disgusting. But I wasn't going to say that, because junkies hate baths. Then I'd taper her down as slowly as I could with the dope I'd bought from Jezebel. After that she'd have to stick it out, because I wasn't buying any more. I'd already made up my mind about that. When she was through with the withdrawal she could work with me, or get a job waiting tables or ringing up sales in Woolworth's, or maybe she could get a job at someplace nice, like Saks or Bergdorf's. She was pretty enough. Or she could leave and go back to Jezebel's or go to college or do whatever the hell else she wanted to do. I'd done my good deed for the day and now it was up to her.

But I didn't say any of that. Instead I said, "Hey. You know, I went out to Westchester. I met your parents."

She froze. She opened her mouth to speak but nothing came out.

"Yeah. And while I was there I broke your neighbor's window."

I looked at her. Her face unfroze and for a short quick moment she was beautiful again, and her lips moved toward something like a smile.

"Oh yeah?" she said.

"Yeah. And if you get yourself cleaned up a little bit we can go back and do it again."

She came closer to a smile. We got out of the car and went to the Sweedmore. Lavinia gave Nadine a sharp look but she didn't say anything. She couldn't; I was probably the only girl in the place paying her rent on time every Friday. But a thousand bucks—seven hundred now— wasn't that much, and I didn't know how much longer that would keep up. We walked up to the third floor. Two girls were coming down the stairs, girls about Nadine's age, laughing and talking a mile a minute about where they would go dancing that night.

"Hey, Joe," one said. "How's it—"

But then she saw Nadine and stopped and they hurried down the stairs.

Nadine looked at them like they were from another planet.

We got to my room and I unlocked the door and went inside. Nadine followed slowly, looking around like something might jump out and bite her.

"This is it," I said. "You can stay here until something better comes along."

"Thanks," she said. "I . . ." She didn't finish her sentence.

I opened the closet door.

"Here. Pick something out. It'll be too big, but it'll fit better than that."

She looked for a minute and then took out a blue dress. It was the one Jim had bought for me. She looked at me.

"That's fine," I said. "You can keep it. I'll be right back."

It was funny, it made me a little nervous, having her out of my sight. Like she might take off and run back to Jezebel's. But so what if she did? If that was what she wanted, there was nothing I could do about it.

I locked the door behind me and went down to the front desk and gave Lavinia a nickel for the phone. I called Shelley.

"She's here," I said.

"Joe, what the hell are you— Oh. Her."

"Yeah," I said. "Nadine. I mean, you said you wanted—"

"No," she said. "I do want to. I do. I'll be right over."

# Chapter Thirty-one

Nadine had put on my blue dress and thrown the clothes from Jezebel's in the trash. She sat on the bed and rubbed her arms, like she was cold. I went into my purse and took out the papers and the works Jezebel had given me. I tossed the works and one paper on the bed next to her.

"Here," I said. I put a record on the phonograph and sat down on one of the chairs. I looked out the window while Nadine did what she needed to do. It took her long enough. Afterward she just sat quietly. One paper wasn't much of a fix for her.

"Where's the bathroom?" Nadine asked. I told her it was down the hall and she stood up. She stopped when she got to the door and looked at me. I thought she was going to say something but she didn't; she turned around and left.

While she was gone there was a knock at the door. It was Shelley. She was all in white again, this time in a summer dress.

Shelley smiled in a kind of shy way, like she had before. "Hey Joe," she said. "Thanks for calling me."

"Come in," I said.

Shelley came in and looked around my room. She looked a little squeamish, like maybe she'd catch something if she touched anything. Like she hadn't grown up in a room just like this one.

"She's here?" Shelley said. She walked around, looking at my things.

"Yeah, she'll be back in a second. Sit down."

She walked over and looked at the record player. "What're you listening to? It's nice."

"Billie Holiday. 'He's Funny That Way.' Something like that."

"Can I turn it up a little?"

"Sure. Go ahead."

Shelley turned up the record loud and then she sat on the bed. I wondered if she would take Nadine home. It would save me a whole lot of trouble, but didn't seem likely. Maybe she would get her a room here at the Sweedmore while she was cleaning up. Give her a little money until she could get a job or whatever she wanted to do.

"You want some coffee?" I asked.

"Okay," Shelley said.

I went to the corner table where the hot plate was. I filled up the percolator from a pitcher of water I kept on the floor underneath.

"You're sure it's the right girl?" Shelley asked.

"Of course," I said. "It's her. Why wouldn't it be?"

Shelley didn't answer me.

I picked up the coffee and a spoon. But then I stopped. The right girl?

Was there a right girl and a wrong girl?

Shelley didn't even know Nadine. What did she care if—

I dropped the coffee on the table.

Oh, Jim. I am so, so sorry.

I started to turn around and there was a loud *crack* and I fell back against the table like I'd been punched.

Shelley had shot me.


*No one had any idea Jim was mixed up in dope again.*

*A long time ago he took some pictures of me—you know, to sell.*

*He said he was gonna get me in pictures. . . .*

*Sometimes he takes pictures of the girls to sell to magazines.*

*Jake Russo, Real Estate . . . rents places all over Manhattan.*

234

*You know, there's a lot of out-of-work actors in this town, Joe. I know people who'd kill for any kind of work.*

*Maybe this wasn't about the drugs, after all. Plenty of people had reason to kill McFall.*

*I've been thinking about Shelley. I'm not sure if you should trust her as much as you do.*

*What did Shelley tell you?*

What did Shelley tell me?

*All I saw was the car. A brand-new Rocket 88.*

I'd thought there was only one person in the world who knew me well enough to make it all work. But there were two. And I'd picked the wrong one.

I'd been wrong about everything. Right from the start, I'd been wrong about it all.

She got me in my side, right at my waist. My dress was torn and I was bleeding. Blood was pouring down my clothes and pooling on the floor.

I felt like I was on fire where I'd been shot.

"Shelley," I said, turning around. My knees were weak. It was hard to stand up. "Shelley. How could you?"

Shelley stood up off the bed. She was holding a gun. It was pointed right at my heart.

My sister.

Now she didn't look like that girl in the paper at all. There was nothing so sophisticated about her now. She was just the same girl I'd always known, the girl who wanted treats from the Automat, the girl who wanted a new dress every year, the girl who always, always, got what she wanted.

And I'd always given it to her. My sister.

"McFall had pictures of you," I said. My mouth was dry and it was hard to speak.

Shelley was angry now. "I needed the money. You were shooting all your dough up your arm and I needed money. That was ten years ago. Last month he calls me up. He kept those pictures, all this time. He was gonna blow my whole career. I paid him off twice but he still wanted more. And that goddamn little prep school whore, she was there the last time I met McFall for a payoff. I don't know why the hell he brought her along. I guess he really had a thing for her."

"Oh, Shelley."

My knees buckled and suddenly everything was sideways. I had fallen down.

The pool of blood on the floor was bigger now.

"You should have taken the jail time," she said. "That's what you were supposed to do. You should have taken the murder rap for McFall and let the girl disappear. You should have let her go. Then I wouldn't have to do this. She probably would've killed herself sooner or later anyway. I wasn't worried about it. But you had to go and find her and bring her back. You had to be the big hero and save the girl."

"Jim was never selling dope at all," I said.

Shelley smiled. "I don't know who McFall ripped off for all that dope, and I don't care. Maybe it was Jim, after all. But I doubt it. I didn't have nothin' to do with that. I just needed to find McFall and get rid of him. Once you started looking around, Joe, once I saw that you weren't gonna let it go, it had to be someone. I knew Springer had a hard-on for Jim anyway. He always has. Anyway, it was you who wouldn't give it up, Joe. It was you who wouldn't do what you were supposed to. All I did was point you in the right direction."

"How'd you know what Springer was thinking?" I asked.

"I still got some friends from the old days," she said. There was something like a smirk on her face. "I'm not stupid, Joe. I know who to stay friends with. Who to stay friends with and who to let go."

So now Nadine had to go, because she knew about the pictures McFall had of Shelley. Because I had tried to save her.

And now I had to go, too. Because I would still try to save Nadine. Because I knew everything.

But those were just excuses. This was just her way to get some use out of me before she got rid of me. I knew the real reason, we both did.

Because every dance lesson she took, every dinner I bought, every new dress she wore, she knew how I paid for it. Because she couldn't bring friends home to a sister who wore short dresses and smelled like cheap perfume. Because every time one of our mother's boyfriends got fresh with her, I should have protected her. Because every time she let the old man at the candy store maul her for a soda, I should have bought her the soda instead. Because no matter how many hours I spent on the street, we still lived in a filthy rooming house. Because when I couldn't stand it anymore and I started sniffing dope to sleep through it all, I gave her even more to be ashamed of. Because even though you can't pay for dance lessons working at Woolworth's, I still should have found a better way. Because after I got hooked on dope, I stopped spending the money on her and spent it on drugs instead. Because she'd had to change her name so no one would know we were related.

Because I was everything she'd come from, everything she never wanted to be.

"Jesus, Shelley," I said.

Shelley walked toward me. "I wouldn't have bothered you, Joe, once you were in the joint. You know, when Jake changed my name for me, he got me a new birth certificate and all that stuff. So no one would have known you were my sister. But I guess it's better this way. You would have found a way to screw things up for me sooner or later."

She crouched down so her face was closer to mine. I never knew how much she hated me until I saw her face right then. "You know, Joe, you never did a goddamned thing for me. You never did nothing for my whole damn life but cause trouble. You know what it was like, coming up, everyone knowing my sister was a whore?" She shook her head. "No, of course you don't. Now for once you're gonna be useful. You're gonna disappear, and I won't ever have to worry about you screwing things up for me again. You're never gonna let me down again."

She was right. I'd never let her down again.

I was burning up where I had been shot.

"When they—" I started coughing again. Blood came out of my mouth and splattered on the floor.

"When they find you?" Shelley said. "You and Nadine? I guess they'll figure they were wrong about Jim

239

after all. I guess they'll figure they were right the first time, that you and McFall were both mixed up in some kind of a dope situation. Or maybe they'll think it was Jim, and he had a partner. Honestly, Joe, I don't care what they think. But they won't think it's me. No one even saw me come up here, except you. We got that old biddy at the desk out at her sister's in Queens. Her sister had a big emergency. And you know, I don't think anyone's gonna worry about it too much. I wouldn't count on making the papers. Two junkie whores gone. It ain't too exciting."

"I'm sorry," I said. "Oh Jim. I'm so sorry."

"What? If you're gonna talk, Joe, you gotta speak up. I can't hear you. It's like that thing they say, speak now or forever hold your mouth, or whatever it is. 'Cause this is it for you, Joe.

"This is it for you, Joe," she said softly.

She poked at me with the gun, and for a second I thought I saw something on her face—something like regret. But maybe it was my imagination.

I was bleeding a lot. I had thought she was going to shoot me again but now I saw that it didn't matter.

I was bleeding a lot. She didn't need to shoot me again.

I heard a man say, "Hey, baby. Everything okay in here?"

My eyes were closed. I forced them open and looked up. It was a man in a pin-striped suit and a gray fedora.

I knew him. He was waiting outside Paul's when I went in. I'd seen him in Katz's. In Bryant Park. In the restaurant where I ran into Shelley. He'd stopped by her table.

Shelley stood up. "Yeah," she said. "I'm just waiting for the other one to come back from the powder room."

"Hey," I said. "I bet you drive a black Chevrolet."

He looked at Shelley. He was a good-looking fellow, but he didn't look nice. His face had deep lines in it and his eyes were set like stone. I wished Shelley could have picked a nicer guy.

"Did she say something?"

"I don't know." Shelley shrugged and started looking around my room. She opened the closet and looked at my dresses. "Look at this trash," she said. "You've always been a dope, Joe, you know that? You've always been a goddamned dope."

I was going to say something, but I forgot what it was. The record kept playing. My eyes closed. It seemed now like it couldn't have happened any other way. Like this was the way it was supposed to be. This was how it had to end. All the disappointments added up to this.

I heard Nadine coming back down the hall. *Don't do that,* I said. *Stop.*

"Why?" It was Monte. He was sniffing a line of dope off the coffee table in our first apartment.

I loved that table. I loved our apartment and everything in it. It was ours. I was finally out of my mother's place and on my own. I was going to have Shelley come and live with us, like a real family, just as soon as we got settled. Monte said everything would be different now. He'd take care of me, me and Shelley, and I'd never have to worry about making money again. I'd never have to let anyone touch me again. He was going to get a job at this factory in Brooklyn where his cousin worked, and he was going to take over paying for Shelley's acting classes, he was going to give her money every week like I'd been doing. It had always been just me and Shelley. We couldn't count on our mother. I worried about her so much that sometimes it hurt. Sometimes I couldn't sleep at night. I loved Monte, but that was the real reason I'd married him. To take care of Shelley.

"It's no good for you," I said. I was seventeen. I knew you could get hooked. But I wasn't exactly sure how.

He leaned back on the sofa and closed his eyes. He looked so happy. "No, it ain't so bad," he murmured.

"Well, then I'm gonna try some." Monte was three years older. He had said that as long as you didn't do it every day, you'd be fine. Nothing bad could happen to you.

I leaned down and took a sniff. It tasted horrible. I felt like I might be sick. I leaned back and curled up against Monte.

"It didn't do anything," I said. I didn't see how anyone could get hooked on the stuff. It tasted awful and it didn't do anything. Except I was starting to feel a little sleepy. And I thought I might get sick. Monte put his arm around me and pulled me close. His hand felt so good on my shoulder.

"Wait," he said. "Just wait. It'll do something."

# Acknowledgments

A million thank-yous to Dan Conaway and Simon Lipskar; to Clara Farmer and everyone at Atlantic Books; and to Jody Hotchkiss and Danae DiNicola.